The SCAM

1/13/12
To Malcolm & Roberta
With my Aloha
BeHejo

THE SCAM

BETTEJO DUX

Library of Congress Data (pending)
Dux, Bettejo.
    The Scam/Bettejo Dux
    ISBN-13: 978-1466371477 (paper)
    ISBN-10: 1466371471
    1. Humorous fiction.

Copyright © 2011 by Bettejo Dux

This is a work of fiction. Names, characters, businesses, organizations, places, events and incidents either are the product of the author's imagination or are used fictitiously. Any resemblance to actual persons, living or dead, events, or locales is entirely coincidental.

All rights reserved. No part of this book may be reproduced in any manner whatsoever without written permission except in the case of brief quotations embodied in critical articles and reviews. For information, address Bettejo Dux at onegeaeme@aol.com.

Author Photo © Arnold Meister
Cover photo © Emily Miller, Kauai – www.beware-the-emily.com
Cover Design Matthew Miller

Dedicated to

Bill and Bomp

In the zoo

"She was much prettier last time," the woman in front of us said.

"Wasn't so damn cold last time," the man alongside her grumbled

"Gets colder every year."

"Ooops! Look out Hattie! Fall down in that and I'll play hell getting you back on your feet."

She was built like a shorter, chubbier, Art Buchwald. He was an underweight Peter Sellers.

The pond was frozen over. It was a thin layer of ice, but strong enough for the waterfowl to walk on.

Just as the lengthy procession crossing the bridge followed each other, two-by-two, so the brightly feathered mallards below us on the surface of the pond followed each other two-by-two. The ducks were more colorful. Winter clothing has a tendency to be drab, but the people had a more interesting way of going. Ice had formed on the path; people slipped, slithered, and slid. The ducks, in contrast, walked sedately.

Only father would have a garden wedding in the snow.

At the head of the overland trekkers was Father, of course, dressed, not quite appropriately, in a white tailored Western suit, very fancy, very expensive, and hand-tooled purple-leather high-heeled boots. His silk shirt was ruffled down the front and at the wrists. He'd not worn his Stetson, at the bride's request, but he did wear his father's silver spurs and a long flowing white wig turned under in a sweeping pageboy at the shoulders.

He was a startling figure of a man; a swinging 20th Century Buffalo Bill with a dash of P.T. Barnum tossed in for good measure.

The little woman at his side, pale as the snow and dressed in yellow lace, was a Dresden doll. She, as Father had announced to the numerous friends and relatives, was our sunshine. I doubt there was any of the real stuff this side of Waikiki.

The sky was a cold wet specter lying ten feet off the ground, descending, mischievously at times, to tweak one's nose with icicle fingers. The Christmas tree forest, where the marriage ceremony was to be performed, appeared and disappeared in the fog, as did the entire wedding procession.

It was a scene right out of an exquisite twelfth century Japanese scroll. Picture it – the arched, ornately carved bridge; the pond, a perfect oval; the staid column of ducks; the long line of people; the misty trees, the fog – all very classical and refined, yes? No.

We were at the tail end of a parade of people passing over the bridge. The bride seemed to have an endless number of friend and acquaintances; we were in her territory. We, David and I, represented Father's entire family. The street outside the Colonel's, Father's, petting farm and zoo, was lined for a half-mile in either direction with an assortment of automobiles as overbearing as the guests.

The bride's black limousine was a solid mass of satin ribbons and rose rosettes. God knows where they got the roses. It looked as though it had just won the Kentucky Derby. Parked outside the main gate, the motor purring and puffing clouds of exhaust, it was primed by the chauffer for a fast getaway.

Only Father's friends in flashy sports cars livened up the party. Ferraris, Porsches, and Jags rubbed bumpers with stately chauffer-driven Bentleys and Cads.

David and I had arrived the day before. We'd been ferried in from the airport in a musty old station wagon which was used to transport food, and, apparently, lovesick lions, to and from the zoo. It was billowy with bits of straw and hay, and fragrant with animals fodder, feces, and fur; by the time we got to Father's place, so were we. I was amazed at David's forbearance.

This vehicle, by the way, on the day of the wedding, was consigned to the garage, just as we'd been consigned to the end of the line.

Ahead of us, David and I watched the bride and groom disappear into the haze. Father had staked a path curved and bound by white ribbons and yellow roses, which he and his bride did their best to follow. The bride, who had swooned twice already, was unsteady on her feet; Father seemed to be holding her up. They were winding, ever winding, like their lives before and behind them, towards the carousel in the forest.

Behind us the scene changed, from the ridiculously sublime to the outrageously bizarre.

Behind us, treading on our tails as it were, was Lulu the llama, her head with its limpid brown eyes and long white lashes, close enough to spit in our faces had we turned around. Behind her were the snowy geese, almost as tall as me, and a worry to Lulu I could tell. Behind them were the big-horn sheep, two ewes, a ram and a pair of lambs, the dogs, one gentle Malamute, with fierce yellow eyes and intelligent wolf mask, two yappy apricot poodles, trimmed in formal French cut and collared in turquoise sequins, and the three Great Pyrenees keeping the flock in line.

The ponies, behind them, picked their way daintily, carefully, across the slippery bridge.

These were not invited guests. This was their territory. We were in the petting zoo, but the animals behaved as well as the people—until the cougars began to roar.

For you see, behind all this, in magnificent cages surrounding the pond, the cougars, their triangular heads resting on crossed paws, lay on lofty perches watching the proceedings. Their eyes were hooded but watchful. Only their tails, slowly twitching, indicated they were living animals. When one of the cats raised her head and roared, the pace on the bridge quickened.

As Lulu nudged us forward at a faster clip, so did we nudge the couple ahead of us.

"Easy now, young lady," the man in front of us said. "It's slippery as hell out here today."

"She married in the spring, I remember now," the lady said. "It was right after Bessie and Owen came back home."

"That the daughter?"

"The very one."

"Every year gets worse," he shook his head.

A light snow began to fall. The familiar strain of Lohengrin's Wedding March pealed forth from the steam calliope in the forest. The ear-splitting sounds of the elegant music, mingled with the cougar roars, pony snorts, geese honks and poodle yaps were more than I could handle. When one of the ducks fell through the ice below us in the pond and began flapping and quacking, it was entirely too much for me. I didn't dare look at David; if we began to laugh it might start a stampede.

I had missed the first wedding, that of Mother and Father, but I was an active participant in this one.

Father

David and I raised three children, a boy and two girls, during the terrible 60's. We lived through more than our share of crashes, bangs, drug scenes and peace protests, psychiatrist's couches, parole officers, fights, frights, and a host of other bad misfortunes too numerous to mention. I remember once, during one of the more mundane of our adventures, one of the kids, a long-haired, draft-dodging kid in the slammer, as I recall, finding and sending to my bewildered parents a bumper sticker which read: REVENGE IS SWEET LIVE LONG ENOUGH TO GIVE YOUR CHILDREN A BAD TIME!

I am and always have been of the persuasion that what this world needs, along with more whales and more elephants, is more laughs, so thoughts like that not only amuse me, they keep me afloat in troubled seas. Still, what I had in mind was David and I living long enough to give our children a bad time. Unfortunately, life, as she has unsheathed her little pink paws for us, has a snarly way of handing us in the future that which we would not have her hand us.

It was our fate to have been sandwiched between two capricious generations.

Two Christmases ago, minutes before my beautiful Mother died, she said, "Remember, Karen, David and I are the only sane members of this family," and, with that as a parting shot she keeled over as good as dead from a massive cerebral aneurism, having the presence and grace, nonetheless, to place her full martini glass carefully on the cocktail table as she fell. She didn't break the glass nor spill a drop.

"A mighty slick passing," my Irish-Jewish-Belarusian husband said. It wasn't until the early hours of Christmas Day when she was officially declared dead that we both began to cry. Mother was the bubble in the level of our lives. How important a leveling device, it would not take us long to discover.

*

I've already described Father as looking like a cross between a seventy-five year old swinger and Buffalo Bill. He's as bald on the top as he is on the bottom, I'm sure, but he wears tailored jeans to cover up the one and Max Factor wigs to cover up the other. Once he said to me, "I had two things going for me as a young man, Karen, I was very intelligent and I was very handsome." And he was. Even when he got to be an old man, old ladies fell for him. Little old ladies coo and make over him. Young women love his stories, his animals, and his courtly ways. The ones in the middle love his bed.

I think, truthfully, Father invented sex after sixty. I think, also, he was mal-imprinted: like the duck that thinks the rooster is his mother.

Congress should erect a statue to him in Washington.

I've got an excellent picture of him seated on a horse. A stuffed horse.

As for his temper, it mellowed some with age. But God forbid you should be on the same continent when he blows. He is Zeus tossing lightening bolts, the great God Jehovah with his fires and floods.

To really know him however, one would to meet him in his natural habitat, his zoo, his Garden of Eden. The favorite toy of a spoiled irreverent old man and the place to which, in all its corkscrew turns, his life has led him.

Like the great God Jehovah, though, he, too, is alone in paradise. David and I live in Hawaii. His grandchildren are leading their own convoluted lives, and his beloved wife is dead. I speak with him frequently when he calls to ask for money. We pay to keep him in his zoo, and if you think it odd we should support Father's extravaganza, look at his way, if we didn't support his zoo there, we would have him, and his zoo, here.

Father, as much as he loves us, has a difficult time sharing the planetary system with us mere mortals.

Father keeps a llama, a matched pair of dapple-gray pygmy horses (mean as hell), parrots, foxes and God-know-what-all else around the place for company.

He picks up nickels, dimes, and folding money showing visitors around the place. It's beautiful, and it makes him feel like a man of independent means. He also gets to behave like the showman he is, his snake-oil patter should be taped and preserved in the Smithsonian.

His last capitol request was for the 'Living Carousel,' equipped with steam calliope. "For the children," Father said. And, although I'd never seen it I had no trouble picturing the old man riding it.

There had not been many carousels in Father's past. His father, the sheriff, had died when he was six leaving him and his mother destitute. Those were not the days to be a poor widow woman with child.

Grandma took in wash and cleaned houses for the rich. Father sold newspapers on windy streets and stole apples from the grocer on the corner. He also shined shoes and ran errands.

He had little, if any, formal schooling. He says he had a third-grade education, but that's probably an exaggeration. Father's been known to make them. However, and I'm sure this is true, school held little charm for him. His enthusiasm for the classroom was under par to say the least. Real life on the streets of town was more adventuresome than life in a stuffy classroom.

He made his first fortune selling cheap vacuum cleaners for fancy prices door-to-door. Then he learned to sell men on the idea of selling vacuum cleaners for him door-to-door. His sales crew would have died for him and he was on his way.

I doubt, in the manner of Adam Smith, he could define the economic system he defended with such bluster and bravado, but he didn't need to define it, he invented it.

He could have taught Adam a few tricks. But all that money he made and lost couldn't buy the little boy he'd been a ride on a carousel.

Let's back up to the last time he lost all his money, on a monkey deal, I think, or was it lobster? Lately all Father's schemes had an animal theme. We'd already gone through turkeys, wild burros, and chickens, which lay colored eggs; they did, when they laid at all, which wasn't often. The eggs, when one boiled them, bounced.

Father would call and demand money. We'd hedge. Then Mother would call, "Karen, don't you dare give him a penny. It's just another one of his hare-brained schemes," and she would spend the rest of the three minutes she'd paid for, tuning me in to their day-to-day chaos, and I would end up sending money. A cashier's check made out to her. She hates it.

We tried to convince her it was entertaining. Life with Father was never dull. Expensive, but not dull.

About six years ago, he began the long economic bottoming out process that would end with yet another bankruptcy. Mother never told us how he lost the money, monkey business or lobsters, but she was mad as hell. It was that collapse that called forth her famous last words.

But the truth, you know, she loved him.

The truth is, we all do.

The end of their life was the full downswing. All the way. They crashed. They burned. The poor house was the real world specter that haunted them at the end. Father used to tell David, "Son, all of us are faced with the same problem. We either live too long or we don't live long enough." Confronted with the somewhat mixed blessing, he picked himself up and started all over again, on David's money, at the ripe old age of seventy-one.

Mind you, he never contributed to Social Security. He considered SS a sinister communist plot; he called them 'common-ists'. His father the dashing sheriff in the wild wild west, it was grandfather's silver spurs he wore at the wedding, had shot his Wobblies, so father knew what that was all about.

His mother, a pioneer woman, had crossed the country in a covered wagon, shooting Indians all the way. I don't know what he made of that. Communism aside, to steal, in Father's lexicon, is good fun. As long as you don't get caught. To take charity is a disgrace.

Unless it's from his daughter.

Holt Camp

David and I live in Hawaii as far away from Father as we can get and still be in the same country. We have a chunk of land on the North shore of Kauai, twenty acres on the water up the coast from the sleepy little town of Hanalei.

Once our itchy-footed youth was spent, David returned to his other love, engineering, and I returned to the land. There was a time in our lives when to watch a plane depart for anywhere without us was a personal insult.

For years we tagged along with Father on his adventures around the world. Me, dropping babies in foreign ports like a mother cat dropping kittens in a drafty barn, and David, who is a graduate engineer, learning about life first hand.

In Indonesia, David was President of an insurance company that sold a ton of policies and flew by night.

In Saigon, we got mixed up with a little gunrunning ring, Father's, and ended up doing some high-class running ourselves. The somewhat other than law-abiding citizens who were after us wanted the operation all to themselves.

But it was Venezuela that put the cork in David's wine. In Caracas, David was President of an oil company Father invented called OILUSA, which was fine. We lived it up – servants, private schools for the children, chauffer-driven cars, and swimming pools – a big one for the adults, a small one for the children – for several years.

Then, at a medal and sash-beribboned embassy-do, David overheard the American first Secretary, a tall elegant man with a fake British accent and an Adolph Hitler mustache, say to his wife, who was rich as Aristotle Onassis and looked like him, too, "I say, sweetness, how does one become President of an oil company at twenty-seven?"

"One's daddy owns the company," his wife brayed.

We were packed and out of there within a week.

"I'm through being Daddy's little boy," David snapped. "Besides the kids are slowing us down. The next time we have to run they'll catch us."

Father hung in there for another six months after we split and sold the oil fields for a cool million, tax free, to a corrupt Paraguayan politico, and got the hell out of there before this man learned Father's oil fields were not only dry, they were non-existent.

That's when Father moved north and became the Colonel.

And David and I moved to Kauai.

David is a businessman, and a good one. He makes enough money designing bits and pieces of things so essential to whatever goes on out in the real world that we, and Father, too, can live the life we choose.

When inflation, or Father, begins to erode too deeply into our healthy bank account, David invents some crazy little something and sells it to somebody, but not to me. I detest machines. My kitchen is late nineteenth century. I even had David design me a hand pump for my water, and it works. I can afford to be eccentric.

We are not hurting for money.

David has a complete shop and office a quarter of a mile from the house, where he walks to work every morning, whistling, minus his shirt. A pleasant walk from the house, on the other side, I have my barn, organic garden, nursery, apiary, orchard, kennel, and a poultry house. Also, an army of beautiful people.

David designed a water system independent of the county, an auxiliary generator which operates a few appliances I will allow - we use candles and kerosene lamps for lighting - and we are never at a loss for strong young backs to generate whatever other types of energy we need. We are nearly self-sufficient. As a matter of fact, we don't really give a damn what Rockefeller or the Arabs do with their oil.

I keep the house free of David's machines. He keeps the house free of my zoo and my plants, which would inundate us, were I to be given free rein. I worship trees. I would have a forest in the living room if I could. Actually, I wanted a house the horses could walk around in, but David balked. Well, I put my foot down when David wanted to install a fancy entertainment center in the house. If we want entertainment in the house, I can think of a dozen other ways to get it. I do not allow radios or television sets on the property.

We don't miss them.

David's family?

Both his parents are dead. He, too, is an only child. His mother was a precious strait-laced Irish Catholic lady who used to say, "I don't know why I like her. She's not a Catholic." She did like me, but she prayed a lot. I'm certain I was the motivating force behind hundreds of votive candles during my mother-in-law's declining years.

To the dismay of the church, when she died, she left all her money to me.

David's father was a gruff old bear who would surely have been a heller had it not been for Mama's velvet curb. He was the Jewish-Belarusian, and a closet bottom-pincher, but I never snitched.

They were the soul of conservatism.

David's parents and my parents detested each other. Each thought the other a flaming example of all the things wrong with the country, and that, as it turned out, was another leveling influence in our lives. David and I were kept so busy keeping the old folks from killing each other we rarely had time, or energy, left to fight with each other. Holidays at our house, traditional gathering days, were filled with sudden stompings-out, flaring-ups, and temper tantrums from the old gentlemen.

The two old ladies spent the entire time out-sniffing each other.

The children, by comparison, were angels.

We were happier when we moved here, two thousand miles away from the whole damn clan. Yet, when his parents died, not only did a great sadness descend on us, so, also, did a great ennui.

That lasted until the children got in the act.

We don't need to browse in the bowels of the Great Open-Air Insane Asylum called radio-television-newspaper land to get our jollies. Our jollies are homing pigeons; they fly home to roost and do other messier things.

For the past year since Mother died, we've had a welcome moment of peace, a flaw in the frayed and tattered fabric of our lives.

And we've loved it.

The children are no longer about the house. At least not all the time. They're grown and gone, Alice to school, Tommy among the radicals, Pat, married to a nice local kid recently released from jail, mother of a brown-eyed hapa-haoli daughter. My granddaughter's other grandmother is pure Hawaiian, which makes Nalani Irish-Jewish-Belarusian-Scottish-Hawaiian-Dane. Already she's an island beauty.

Come the Revolution we need have no fear; we're related to every dissident in the state.

I don't worry about the children out in the cold cold world. I worry about the world.

For many moons we had but one worry, Father. In his grief, which was awesome for the first year, he was easy to handle. Serenity descended.

I should have known it couldn't last.

*

New Years came and went; we don't pay much attention to it in these parts. I don't own a calendar and half the people in the camp neither know what year it is, nor care.

The day the trouble started was the day before somebody invaded somebody and the day after somebody invaded somebody else. We don't take the papers, as you know, and I try not to read one even when I see one. On this day, Gypsy Jake, who appears periodically with his violin, burst into the barn. He was aglow with love, joy, and glad-tidings for all.

Jake was our Get Ready Man, only the theme of his madness was - rejoice, for the end of the world is upon us.

With Jake it was not important one repent. It was only important one cheer.

From the corner of the barn where I stood, I could see the edge of our sandy beach. It ran along outside the dark shadows of the tree line. The Pacific was so blue you could dip a pen in it and write a letter. There was no surf. Brilliantly painted surfboards stood on guard against the trees, and a number of nude brown bodies lay scattered haphazardly about. No one seemed to have paired up that day. I could see two dark-brown coconut heads swimming out to sea.

Further down the beach, I caught a glimpse of the red and gold sails of a sunfish skimming the shore. David was not in his office. When his mind gets too full of pumps and pipes and patents pending he closes shop, takes off his shorts, if he happens to have them on, and goes sailing. On really good days, when his head is spinning, we go out in the sloop and beat up the coast to the valley, or run lazily down to the bay.

A bright red cardinal slashed through the pines, a dog barked, a rooster crowed, and a horse nickered softly from his stall.

Over in the camp the kids were snoozing, or making love, or baking, or reading, anyway they were quiet. They're the best neighbors we ever had. All was well in my world.

Almost all. Alexander, my tall bay gelding, had thrown a shoe and come up lame. Nothing to worry about, but a nuisance. The blacksmith works a Polynesian schedule; Alex might get another shoe next week, or the week thereafter, or maybe four days after New Year next year. Jake was chattering like a magpie and hopping about. He had a well-systemized fantasy going which had to do with the Catholics, and the Baptists, and the Muslims, getting it on and bringing down Armageddon. It made as much sense as anything else in this crazy world, so I always listened politely, which made him happy and kept Armageddon from happening right here in our barn, I'm sure.

Jake was really rattling about in his cage, that day, and Alex, cross-tied, with a sore foot, was beginning to worry. Jake was flashing a newspaper back and forth under his nose.

"Jake" I said, "give me that paper before you give Alex the colic. Can't you see he has a sore foot?" This was right up Jake's alley; he was also a healer, he said. So, while I took the paper and tried not to read yesterday's news, Jake laid hands on Alex's hoof. The wrong hoof, Alex did not look pleased. He laid back his ears and went after Jake with teeth bared, a vicious bite had it connected, but it didn't. Alex isn't mean. He was simply tired of this funny man bouncing around and his foot hurt.

"Play him a song, Jake. He loves Old Black Joe. That's as good as laying on the hands, isn't it?" Jake, still babbling to himself, dropped Alex's hoof. I winced for the horse. Jakes opened his violin case, took out his battered fiddle, and began to play.

Alex relaxed. Me, too.

If one has to read the newspaper the long covered porch that runs the length of the barn, is the best place in the world to do it. Only the sound of nature, the ocean gently lapping, the wind softly moving the trees, and Jake and his squalling violin disturbed the peace of the day. I seated myself on a canvas deck chair and pondered the mess the world was in. Everything in that paper could have been happening on Alpha Centauri as far as I was concerned.

When Jake began to play, some of the bodies on the beach got up, discreetly covered themselves, and headed towards the barn. They even put zoris on. I'm a bitch about wearing shoes around the barn.

The kids, who live in the trees, and on the beach, and in the water, loved Jake. He was an element, too. They were tolerant, patient, and kind. They'd sing Old Black Joe; they were beginning to sing now. Jake knew only three songs, and he sang them over and over until it nearly drove me mad.

When the phone rang, he hardly missed a beat. I don't know how many times I've threatened to take out the damn phone. I dislike phones, but David likes to call me from the office, and I like to talk to him, so I let it stay. Maybe I should consider an intercom system, two tin cans and a long string; David can design something.

Anyway, rather than further disturb the scene, I picked up the phone on the next ring. The kids and Jake picked up Old Black Joe-baby where they'd dropped him, his head all bendin' low and I said, "Hello?"

"Hello, kitten," said the voice on the other end of the line. I could hear the crackle of a long distance connection.

"This is a collect call," the operator began, "will you accept the charges?"

"She most assuredly will," Father replied.

"Yes," I sighed, and, out-classed, out-numbered, and out-sung, the operator hung up.

"Father?"

"None other, baby. How's my favorite daughter?"

Favorite? I'd been under the impression all these years I was his only daughter. I ignored the gambit.

"Fine," I said.

Ah," said Father.

"Ah? What does that mean?"

"Where are you?"

"In the barn. Where are you?"

"Here. How are things in beautiful Hawaii?"

"Beautiful."

"What are you doing?"

"Talking to you."

"Ah."

"Father, are you in the hospital?"

"In the hospital? What makes you ask a question like that?"

"Say 'ah'."

"That's funny, Karen. You always make me laugh. No. No hospital. I suffer from glowing good health." Something was beginning to smell fishy. Father was not always so coy about getting to the point, which, of course, was always money.

"You sound chipper. How are the animals?"

"Eleanor is in heat."

Eleanor is one of the cougars. He has three. All females. When one comes in heat, they all come in heat, in cats it seems to be catching, and it's very noisy. "I know," I said. "How do you get any sleep?"

"It doesn't bother me, kitten."

"It bothers your neighbors. Johnson or Jackson or whatever the man's name is called David three times last week and raised the roof."

"With David?"

"He tried."

"Tell David not to worry. I told Johnson-his name is Johnson, Joseph, I believe-yes, it is Joe Johnson-that I was a warlock and if he complained one more time I'd stick pins in his picture."

"Did it work?"

"Of course. Now he thinks I'm crazy. You don't fool around with crazy old man. You know that."

"Do I ever. Is there a reason for this call, Father, or is this an expensive chat?"

"I enjoy chatting with my daughter."

Particularly if she's paying the bill. I bit my tongue. "Father, look, I have a lame horse."

"For God's sake, Karen, don't let one of those dummies out there touch him. I'll send Calvin."

"You'll send Calvin and Calvin will send the bill. The vets out here are good men and your know it. Anyway, it's not an emergency, he just threw a shoe."

"You have impossible ferriers."

"You know you absolutely adore Ralph."

"Ralph? Who's Ralph?"

"Oh, Daddy, look, I'm already envisioning this bill, Jake is singing "Old Black Joe" and if he doesn't stop I'm going to scream. What is it you want?"

"Jake? Who's Jake? You surround yourself with the strangest people."

I groaned. I nearly screamed. "What is it you want?" I was tempted to say, "How much do you want this time?" But that would start a ten-minute lecture from the Colonel.

"Now don't you worry about the bill. That you're not to do. Things are really looking up for your old father. I expect any minute to be able to pay you both back. With interest."

"There isn't that much money."

He chuckled. "Will you promise me something?"

"What?"

Here began the oldest telephone game. It is rarely cheaper to promise than not to promise, but over the years I've learned a few tricks of my own. Wheedling a promise out of me can take ten minutes. A promise from Father is not worth the wind it's carried on, but a promise from his daughter is another bucket of money. His daughter keeps her word. "I promise."

"Good. I want you to stay right where you are for the next few minutes."

"Stay where I am?" This was going to be easy.

"By the phone."

"We haven't got a long extension cord. While I'm talking to you I can't go far."

"You don't understand. I'm going to hang up and call you back. In exactly…set your watch…"

"You mean the gold Rolex you bought me that I just received the bill for? Father you should not be so generous."

"Nothing's too good for my favorite daughter."

There it was again. "Father?"

"In five minutes I'm going to call you back. Be there."

"Why?"

"You'll see. I've got a surprise for you."

"A surprise?"

"I've arranged a conference call. Someone else will be on the line with me that I want you to talk to. And be nice to."

"Who?"

Father has many tones of voice. He's an expert screamer when he wants his way, which is always. He can wheedle, weasel, and woof with the best of them. He's a shouter and a shaker and one who stirs things up, but his present tone was a new tone, I could not place it.

"Just someone, kitten," his voice was so gooey you could put it on toast and eat it.

"Father?"

"Promise you'll be there, baby, that's all I ask."

"I promise." You notice I hadn't promised to answer the phone. I'm not my father's daughter for nothing.

"Good baby. I'll get right back to you."

I put the phone back on the hook and opened the paper. I had no idea what Father was up to, but I was certain it would upset my life a lot more than whoever was invading whoever out there in cloud-newspaper land.

"Jake! Kids! Please try Danny Boy. Or the other one. I know you know another one." The kids and Jake, softly now, began to sing and play "Three Blind Mice."

Alex was asleep.

Jenny Fisher

I hadn't promised to answer the phone, but I did. My Father knows exactly how to pique my curiosity. When the phone rang I leaped for it.

The kids and Jake ignored the jangle, the mice were running, the carving knife chopping.

It was a mixed-up conversation, the three of us talking over each other half the time. I caught the lady's name when Father introduced us, Jhon-vieve, in the French style, not Genevieve as in sweet.

"Jhon-vieve?" I said.

"Just call me Jenny, dear. Jenny Fisher."

"Jenny Fisher?" I said.

The conversation proceeded a bit faster with Jenny in command. I did most of the listening. I was no match for her. She sounded sweet and nice, but I was in shock when the conversation ended. The phone dangled at the end of the cord for several minutes before I had the presence to replace the cradle. I'd been sitting very tensely, my neck was stiff and one foot had gone to sleep. I shook it awake. It was quiet in the barn. Alex, mesmerized beyond recall, had the walleyed stares. He'd gone to that place where all good horses go who have heard Three Blind Mice once too often.

The kids and Jake had disappeared.

I unhooked Alex from the crossties, removed his halter and shooed him into his stall. It was two-feet deep in clean fresh-smelling straw and he wasted no time getting a load off his feet. He settled into his bed, nose deep, with a contented 'oof', and went back to dreamland. I gave him a pat on his knobby head and left him in the happy-hunting ground, closing and latching his door, and set out for the house.

The sand and the sea were so inviting I cut through the pines and walked homeward along the beach. The kids must have gone into town or back to camp for they were not in sight. I could see the Sailfish, so I guessed David was either halfway to the bay or back to the office.

It was a beautiful afternoon. There was only one disturbing sight, Gypsy Jake, with shoes on, a rarity all by itself – I could see their dark soles lifting and falling in the sand, violin case in hand – was scurrying in a decidedly curious fashion up ahead of me on the beach.

It was the last I was to see of Gypsy Jake.

*

Eons ago, during the marches and protests and hand-wringing war in Vietnam, a dear Quaker lady used to say to me, "When I don't know what to do, Karen, I bake cookies. I can do that."

At the meetinghouse on Oahu, we had nervous breakdowns with the best of them, but we ate well. Ann's cookies were the talk of the town and we shared them with the cops who came to arrest us, the agents who came to spy, and the Young Americans for Freedom who came to sneer.

From Ann I learned the value of baking when confronted with emotional turmoil. My specialty, however, is banana bread. And not any old banana bread, either. I bake consecrated banana-macadamia-nut-raisin heavy-as-a-brick bread. Baked with love and freshly ground whole-wheat flour, it is a favorite treat in times of crisis. I picked some over-ripe bananas off a tree on my way back to the house, found my way, distractedly, into the kitchen, and commenced to fill it full of delicious smells.

By the time David got home from work a couple of hours later, I was dancing around my friendly kitchen singing like a bird.

David, like me, had walked home along the beach. I'd followed his perambulations from the kitchen window. Something about our beach makes people stumble through it like parboiled drunks. It's the "three steps to the right, one step to the left, hunch, shake your fanny, Holt Beach Scramble," and David's innovations on this day were pretty classy. He'd have a pocketful of shells, beach glass, and driftwood to bestow on me when he got in the door.

"Empty your pockets! Better yet take your pants off. Be sure to wipe the sand off your feet."

"Some damn homecoming," David yelled from the porch. He dropped his shorts inside the door, wiped his feet on them, they were brown and sandy colored for that reason, and entered the kitchen bare as a furry egg. "I brought treasures. What's that smell? He sniffed the air. "Banana bread?" He laid a king's ransom of junk on the kitchen counter. A lot of it spilled off onto the floor.

"You love it, you know you do."

"I do." He gave me a deep wet kiss.

"It's not too warm. Not too cold. Just right. Want milk? Or wine?"

"You. Oh. Oh. Better make that wine. These are macadamia nuts."

One day I must make David some macadamia nut bread when I don't have something devastating to tell him.

"It's not that bad, darling."

"How bad?"

"Father called."

"Oh, balls," David said. "I thought it was going to a real pisser. Macadamia nuts. What'd we do, run out of walnuts?"

He settled himself carefully on a kitchen stool, his penis peering out of its furry nest like a newly hatched snake in a hen house.

"How much does he want?"

"How much what does he want?"

"Money. Lucre. Greenbacks. Benjamin's. That stuff we keep pouring down that bottomless pit we call a checking account."

"He doesn't want money."

I'll give him credit, he didn't choke, but he looked at me oddly and cautiously took another bite of bread. He took another swallow of wine to wash it down. "He just wants you to pay for the phone call?"

I laughed. "I'm sure we'll get the tab. The last time he paid a bill Roosevelt was in office."

"Which Roosevelt?"

"And it'll be a dilly. It was a combination call."

"What the hell is a combination call?"

"It's when more than two people are hooked into the conversation."

"Say what?"

"There were three people on three separate phones in three different parts of the country on one line."

"You. Your Father. And who else?"

"A lady."

"How could you tell?"

"A woman. Jhon-vieve Fisher."

"Jhon-vieve for Christ's sake."

"Jhon-vieve-call-me-Jenny Fisher."

"Young or old?" He was suspicious again.

"Old. She says she's seventy-five. Didn't sound it."

He calmed down and began munching. "What was she selling?"

"She wasn't selling anything. I think she was buying. Well maybe selling a little bit. Let's say they were doing some horse trading."

"Karen stop it. Sometimes you're as bad as your Father."

"Okay. Okay. They want to get married."

David can keep his cool, but the truth is, he did choke on that one.

"Married?"

"Yep."

"How will he support her?"

"Funny. That's exactly the same question I asked."

We sat together at the kitchen bar, a singular pair, David with his bare front, me, in my huge blue baking apron with the bare backside, munching and sipping wine. Two old warhorses, with their heads over the stable door, watching the armies assemble.

"Well," David said at last, "We can always look at it this way…"

And I swear we said it together, "…we're not gaining another mouth to feed, we're gaining another mother."

*

The next few days were so gloriously golden and soft that could we have bottled them we'd be rich as Jackie over night.

Father called four times in three days, and once so distracted he forgot to reverse the charges, and carried on like a lovesick teenager.

I was happy for him. He'd suffered this past year without my mother. We worried we would lose him somewhere along the way. He wouldn't eat. He took no interest in life. I worried that he was forgetting to feed those damn lions. I could see the headlines:

OLD MAN EATEN

BY HUNGRY CATS

His and Mother's years together had been bumpier and more tumultuous than most, but they'd survived. Fifty years of scrapping, loving, raising me, raising hell, wandering this planet, a crusty pair of freebooters, his marriage was his greatest, perhaps his only accomplishment, and it almost killed him.

But the more I heard about his new love the more cheerful I became. She came from a good family. She had a fat bank account. Lots of land. She had one daughter, my father's other favorite daughter. A very successful son-in-law, President of this, chairman of that, Commodore of the local yacht Club. David's ears perked up. It would be fun to have another sailor in the family.

They sounded a bit straight for our tastes, but what the hell. We weren't marrying them. If they came calling, I could out-strait-lace any dozen of them with one hand tied behind my back. I hadn't been David's mother's daughter-in-law for nothing. We might have to perform a fast cover-up at the camp, and David might have to wear clothes – me, too – but we could, if Father's future depended on it, pass.

The only thing that really worries me was what that poor dumb lady was getting into. How long would it be before she discovered she was married to America's Number One Snake-Oil Salesman? How could she handle all those creditors? My mother used to take after them with a broom. At the wedding, instead of rose petals, they could have a ticker-tape parade of unpaid bills.

Should we make one last Herculean effort to clean up Father's stable and pay all those bills? The postage alone would break us.

She said she was seventy-five, perhaps all her faculties had failed. Maybe she wouldn't live long enough to discover the rogue buried not too deeply beneath that adorable façade. One thing was certain, however, she was grown up. Several years ago when Father's star began its descent, Mother, bless her soul, had insisted – since David and I had begun to support them in earnest – that they deed their land to us.

"That way," Mother said, "you'll be acquiring an asset and not pounding sand down a rat hole." Mother, all by herself, was a quaint and crusty old soul.

But it would be a relief not going through probate. If all his angry creditors were to descend on us after his demise, it would take the National Guard with bayonets to hold them back.

It's difficult to describe this trait of my Father's. He is not a dead-beat, at least not run-of-the-mill. But when it comes to paying bills, he is, on principle, against it.

"They have more money than I have, Karen," he always said.

David and I managed, somehow, to keep up with his current indebtedness. At least all of it we knew about. Father is cute about hiding it. He thinks because we pay our bills we suffer from a most severe character flaw. He's tried, ever since he's known David, to break him of this pernicious habit.

Father's monthly bill would have kept Gypsy Jake in food, clothing, and catgut for a whole year. Father knows everyone. Everywhere. And he likes to talk on the phone. He calls it, 'keeping in touch'.

I don't know what it keeps him in touch with, but it keeps us in touch with the poorhouse.

I didn't get a speech. He chuckled. I knew he was up to no good. "Now, kitten, don't give your old dad a short count. I got a deal. Get you and David off the hook, pay you back, with interest, marry my new lady and turn over a new leaf."

"In whose checkbook? I'm still worried about your creditors."

"The land will never come back into my name."

"Not in your name? Whose name will it go into?"

"Don't worry your sweet little head about that. Just sign the papers."

"Father are you going soft in the head? One does not give one's land away."

"I gave it to you."

He had me there.

"And David promised." Years ago. We were at the present time financially into that land up to our ears. "Father…"

"Promise, kitten. Promise. I'll have the papers in the mail tomorrow. We're forming a trust. You'll see. You'll still be my heir. Can't ask you and David to support me and my bride. I must be my own man. Believe me it's the only way. Promise me."

"I promise," I said. My head was spinning. "I'll talk to David."

"I'll talk to David." The Colonel said and slammed the phone in my ear.

I had a riddle for David when he came home that night. "Name one nut more expensive than a macadamia nut. You have thirty seconds."

He got it in two.

*

Don't ask what transpired on that call between Father and David. I don't know. I don't want to know. I do know David arrived home in a perfectly foul mood. He slammed the kitchen door, took several quick swings around my cold, barren kitchen – I'd been in no mood to bake - grinding gritty grains of sand into my beautiful oil-teak floor.

"Put your pants on, Karen. Let's go see Lorraine."

The shorts I had on were adequate, but I did slip on a pair of zoris and a clean shirt.

David went as he was.

*

Lorraine owns and runs a bar just outside of town. She's one of the best friends we have and her bar, the New Papeete, has got to be the greatest place on the island to sit and sip a few.

We love its authentic Tahitian shabbiness. Everything slightly beat and battered, chairs with wobbly legs and hard wooden seats that get more comfortable and stable the longer you sit. Blowfish, and conch shells, woven and fringed palm leaves, and ti-leaf décor, it adds up to all that's left of real island hospitality; the one place in the world where the real spirit of aloha survives.

Lorraine is the mother of the world. We can talk to her about anything, and, after a few of her generous drinks, we usually do. That night was no exception.

It was a quiet night at the New Papeete. The sky was gray and overcast. It was going to rain. It was a Monday night and most of Lorraine's habitués stay home on Monday, recovering from Thursday night, Friday night, Saturday and all day Sunday. In true Polynesian style, on Tuesday and Wednesday they work.

With few interruptions then, David, Lorraine, and I sat on her poster-bedecked verandah overlooking the only road through town. Across the narrow two-lane street what remains of our lowland jungle, tangled hao, koa, and thick tendrils of dripping philodendron, rattled in the wind. Someone had shot out the streetlights, no car passed, not a star peeped through the drizzly cloud-cover overhead. Had it started to rain on Lorraine's tin roof, I swear Sadie Thompson and a gang of rowdy sailors would have come laughing through the rain to join us.

David told the story. I spoke very little. Lorraine listened attentively. Solemnly. Her great intelligent brown eyes moved sadly from David to me, like someone watching a geriatric tennis match. She'd nod, or heave a sigh, or take a deep breath. She knows and adores my father. She and Mother had been the friendliest of rivals. At last, and it was unlike Lorraine – I've never heard her say an unkind word about anybody – and so unexpected, considering the tale David had told she said, "That sounds like one bod lady fo' me."

We were too stunned to comment. We had one more drink, in deep silence, all of us. When we left, Lorraine took us both to her great motherly bosom, nearly suffocating me with her wonderful flower-scent, kissed us both on the cheek in the French fashion and bid us good night.

"Not to worry," she said. "Lorraine feex up everyt'ing honky-dory."

We smiled and waved as we drove away. The headlights, when David turned them on, did not brighten the landscape. As we drove off David said, "Now what in the hell do you make of that?"

*

I'll tell you what I make of that. I'd never tell David, he wouldn't understand. When it comes to crystal ball gazing, David, as well as Lorraine and me, has his own idiotsyncracies. He does a trip called Kepnor-Tregoe. A reasoning man's crystal ball that bogs me down with numbers and weights and ciphers, but it works for David.

I don't know what works for Lorraine. She is an island primitive, and pagan magic, I know, is loose in her head. But I will tell you what works for me.

First of all, I really don't care to know what the future may bring. I prefer to be surprised. What I do want to know, however, is how to handle it. The future can hand me anything, it always has, and since I'm still here to talk about it, I must assume, in my own convoluted way, that I handled it, if not wisely, at least adequately.

Maybe it's the ambience of the island, the magic of Polynesia, or, perhaps it's my ego, but, in my well-ordered fantasy-land, good health, agelessness, serenity, yoga, and my own particular brand of crystal ball gazing, the I Ching, go hand-in-hand-in-hand-in-hand-in hand. One of our kids, Alice it was, gave me the book years ago and taught me how to use it. I keep it with my underwear, the coins, too, three shiny new Lincoln pennies, and I consult it during moments of crisis. It has never lied to me. God knows it's had enough opportunities.

Leaving David and Lorraine to their own devices, the day after our conversation at the New Papeete, I fasted, rode Malcolm, Alex's hoof was still ouchy, stood on my head for half an hour, and threw the coins.

The wonderful part of all this is that evening, by the fire in our huge moss-rock fireplace, David told me the conclusion he and Kepnor-Tregoe had reached.

It was the same advice the oracle had given me.

•

"Karen?"

"Yes, David?"

"I've reached a conclusion."

"Oh, what about, darling?"

"Now look here damn it, you know damn well about what."

"No levity?"

"No levity. No giggles. This is the way we're going to handle your father."

"We can't discuss it?"

"Sure we can discuss it, but we're going to do it my way. I have my reasons."

I nodded. "You don't want to discuss them?" I was as unsure about Kepnor-Tregoe as he was about me and the I Ching.

"No. Not my reasons."

"Okay. I'm ready to listen."

"First we wait for his letter. Right now we know nothing. We do not have enough information to make a decision right now."

Good. The I Ching said precisely the same thing to me. I threw WuWan with only one changing line. "It is not favorable," said the Oracle, " to have in view any goal."

"And then?"

"And then, depending on what transpires, no, no matter what transpires, we handle the old goat with kid gloves. If anything looks fishy we delay. Head him off."

"And how do you propose to do that? We'll have him smack in our laps. He'll fly over here on our, your, money. Demanding. Screaming. Shouting."

David stared at the fire. "He's a civilized man. Intelligent. He'll listen to reason."

"Sure he will. And I'm going to insist he listen to reason in your ear. Not mine. I've already half deaf from insisting he listen to reason."

Outside, the pines, goaded-on by the wind, pushed spider fingers along the windows. It was still drippy and drear. No big storm, that would have been fun, just a steady, dull, London fog drizzle.

An Indian fire burned slowly in the fireplace and David and I, snuggled together on our sinfully expensive rug, could not have been warmer had we been clothed.

"David," I murmured.

"Yes," he answered in my ear.

"There is a conclusion we could reach."

"A couple of conclusions maybe. It could be a long night."

And neither of us thought about Father, or Jenny, for quite a long time.

Trouble

If anyone tells you it doesn't rain in the islands, know him for what he is: a liar. All it did for the next six days was rain. That, of course, is what keeps our garden green. The mountains that ring our valley wept spectacular waterfalls and thick gray clouds rolled and tumbled down the valleys like monster tears.

It was too wet to ride, but there was plenty of work to be done. Keeping a barn full of horses happy and amused in inclement weather is a time-consuming task. I hang their toys, empty Clorox bottles, bright balloons, and basketballs, from lintels over their stall doors, and they bat them back and forth to distraction until that begins to pall. Then I turn on the sound system, my horses are music lovers, all of them, and they bat away in time to the music while I clean stalls.

On a rainy day it's a good idea to stay out of my barn if your stomach is weak. On a rainy day you can get seasick watching all those bouncing balls.

I clean stalls. Brush horses. Talk to them. Sing. I'm not above batting a few balls myself, anything to keep the animals amused. There is nothing worse than a barn full of bored horses.

All animals love the rain. Dog, chickens, birds, ducks, especially ducks, even cats and kittens revel in it. They are joyful when it rains. It's as though, with all mankind locked up somewhere in dry shelters, cars and bars and beds, the world belongs to them. In my opinion the world would be a better place if it would rain all the time.

If the horses could get out in it, they'd love it, too, but I'm vain about my barn. A barn full of mud rollers does nothing for my digestive system. So, they were locked up in their dry snug beds, and I was locked up with them.

The ocean was an unwashed slate, flat, and ugly. We were still not getting any surf. All of us, not only the horses, trod the edge of terminal tedium. Kids from the camp were hanging around the barn because it was a warm, dry spot, but they tried to be helpful. Two hulking surfers from the West Coast helped me pull Alex's other three shoes off. He might as well be comfortable.

A couple of girls, who knew their way around a barn, burnished, brushed, and curried the ponies until they glistened. One girl-Cindy, I think was her name, a black girl from Washington, D.C., she left the next day and missed all the excitement-knew how to do that fancy dressage braid with beads, only Cindy used shells, and my Shetland stud looked fit enough for Madison Square Garden.

We had, at the time, living in assorted tents and tree houses, the entire Junior American Olympic Skiing Team. They were in the island for a short winter holiday, and they found us. These girls with pitch forks and shovels were a caution. The old barn had never been so clean or so full of dandied up horses.

Everyone was here but dear old Jake. I don't like to admit it, but I missed him. We tried a couple of bars of Old Black Joe, but without Jake and his violin it fell flat; even old Alex wasn't amused, and it doesn't take much to amuse Alex.

We kept productive and busy.

We had almost a whole week of drizzle before the big blow struck. I couldn't complain that my batteries hadn't been charged.

*

The letter arrived the same day the front moved in. The surf was enormous. Some of the temporary shelters in the camp blew down. The rain was cold wet knives slashing and the trees were snapping back in self-defense. David and I, together with a committee of kids, had set up temporary beds, sleeping bags, pillows, blankets, and mattresses, across our expanse of living room. It looked the way a High School gymnasium looks during a disaster.

The fire in the fireplace was bigger now and put out a lot of heat, thanks to one of David's inventions I would allow in my house. The house was a big warm cave. Warm with kids. Warm with voices. Warm with laughter, love and peace.

The kitchen was a steaming caldron of good things to eat. I have no trouble understanding the appeal of an extended family. All those nice young kids, and some not so young, helping each other, making room, baking bread, napping, reading, singing, were appealing as hell.

And I, the mistress of this fey castle, snuggled in my California king-size waterbed with a good book and a glass of red wine, lay back and let the world float by.

Then the phone rang.

*

Father had not only sent us the document, he'd also sent Kuuipo - Postmaster and chief practicing shrink of the local Post Office - a letter, asking him, Kuuipo, to call us when it arrived.

I unbundled myself from my warm nest, rebundled myself for the great downpour, and drove off to town. I could barely see the curves in the road.

Kuuipo apologized for dragging me out on a day like this, but, he explained, "It must be important. The Colonel never did this before." Which was true, he'd done other things though, such as sending us a dozen Dungeness crabs, which he knew we adore, but not bothering to see if we were home to collect them. That shut down the Post Office for three days. Bills and letters left town weeks later still smelling like rotten fish.

Another time when our phone was out, Father called Kuuipo collect and sent him to our house, four miles away, in a driving rain storm and riding his bike, to tell us the pygmy mare had foaled. But Kuuipo, like everyone who knows my Father, adores him. If Father says 'jump' Kuuipo bounds. I picked up the letter, threw the Postmaster a big smile, and drove home, good girl that I am, without peeking. That was part of the plan, too. I went directly to David's office. We opened the envelope together.

*

It was a thick envelope. Plain white. No return address. Inside there were two documents. No trust. No corporate papers. No will. One of the papers was a long yellow form describing the land in legal terms, with two blank spaces at the bottom where David and I were to sign.

The document had already been signed by two people we'd never heard of, the people to whom the land was to be given.

The other document was a brown-jacketed Title Deed from an Escrow agent, which, again, was signed by the lucky mystery couple and again had two blank spaces f or us to sign. Together with our signatures this document demanded seventy-five dollars, to be made out to the Escrow Agent, for the privilege of giving my Father's beautiful land away.

"He's really gone soft in the head," I said.

"Try it in reverse," David said but I was not in the mood to laugh.

I don't know that David knew what I was about to do, but he didn't try to stop me. I picked up the phone and dialed information, asked a question, got an answer. Hung up and dialed again. When the party on the other end answered I said, "Mrs. Woodsbury? Is Mrs. Fisher there?"

"No she isn't," replied the voice. It was one of those blowsy hail-fellow-well-met voices that some women acquire as they trample though life, cheery, but somehow threatening, and an ear-buster by phone.

"Do you know when she'll be back?"

"This isn't her phone. Would you like her number?"

"Are you her daughter?"

"Yes I am. Can I help you with anything? Is something wrong?"

"No. Nothing. I'll call back."

Solving the mystery couple had taken me five minutes. I was shaking so hard I dropped the phone. I didn't swear. I picked the phone back up and slammed it in the cradle hoping the crash would burst the lady's eardrums. Then I turned the air blue.

"Good shot, Karen. You deserve a medal." I was still swearing. "He wants to give his land to his new girl friend's daughter. Swell."

I stopped swearing and started to cry. "He wants a divorce, David."

David nodded.

"But he doesn't want to hurt my feelings by asking for one."

David snorted. "Since when did your father ever care about anybody's feelings but his own?"

"They why didn't he tell us who they were?"

"Why create a scene?"

I don't cry often but when I do it's a tropical cloud burst. In seconds I dehydrate myself. My nose turns red and my eyes get puffy. There are some guileful ladies who cry soft and gentle lady-like tears, but I am not one of them. I blubber. I bawl. I bleat. It never fails to bring out the best in men. They become all knights in shining armor. The uglier I get the more courtly they get. I should give it all up and get old and fat and ugly and cry all the time. David held me in his arms-hell, he held me up- I could barely stand. He whispered in my hair, he stroked my back, he patted my fanny, his hands were busy everywhere. "Look, Karen, it may not be as bad as it seems. I'll admit your father does some strange things but this isn't like him. You don't suppose…"

"Don't suppose what, David?" I hiccupped.

"It's only a feeling I have. I could be wrong. But this smells funny."

"Smells," I agreed.

"Hush now, child. Hush. Let me think. They want something. They're after your father's money."

"My father doesn't have any money."

"But he does have land. They're after his land."

"And he doesn't seem indisposed to giving it away."

"Let's reserve judgment on that. You run back to the house like a good girl. Leave the papers here. Dry out. You're wringing wet. Wash your face. Pull up your socks. Have a stiff one. I'll be home shortly."

So while David commenced to Kepnor-Tregoe this one, I threw the I Ching.

We lived to rue the day.

*

The decision, like Gaul, was divided into three parts. First, we would not let Father know we knew to whom the land was to be given.

That was the easy part.

The second part, a plea for delay, was harder. The two of us, David at the office, and me at the barn, arranged our own conference call. Arguing together, Father in the middle, we set out to convince him he must postpone the wedding. He wanted to get married next week. We insisted we had only his best interest at heart. We loved him and we wanted to see him happily married. We waxed eloquently about the forthcoming nuptials. We thought up a hundred reasons, marriage plans, parties, showers, invitations, announcements, any reason to postpone. And, since a love as true and pure as his and Jhonvieve's could do nothing but bloom more fully as the days flew by, he should wait. We'd bring flowers. Macadamia nuts. We fought brilliantly and we won. Three weeks. On her wedding day, three weeks from today, we promised we would do as he requested, give the land as a wedding gift from Mother. In three weeks, we swore on Mother's memory, we would sign the papers giving the land away.

Father was not happy, "I'm eighty years old, Karen, and I only have three weeks to live," he said. But he was compliant.

Exhausted, David and I hung up, on him, and on each other, and headed back towards the house.

We trudged up the beach, David to the east, me to the west, like two tramps at the close of a weary day, or strays in search of shelter from the night.

The wind and rain had gone away, the kids had gone back to camp. The setting sun shone on us anyway.

The next day, early, I instigated the third maneuver.

It took some doing to find a detective recommended in the I Ching, but with a little imagination I read that in the message. I don't know how David and Kepnor-Tregoe managed, but that was our plan. Again I called mainland information, and, armed with a multitude of numbers, began ringing up detective agencies in Father's vicinity. I made a dozen calls before I hit pay dirt. The secretary who answered the phone was polite, obviously well trained, and business-like. She took my name and phone number, seemed interested that I was calling long distance, and put me through to Mr. Adams.

At the other agencies it had been a toss-up, Squeaky Fromm answered one time, Phyllis Diller answered the next. I spent a bundle that day sitting at the other end of a silent phone, neither Squeaky nor Phyl seeming to care that mine was a long distance call.

Mr. Adams, too, at the AAA Detective Agency in Portland, sounded quite professional. His vocabulary and diction were excellent. He was, if anything, pedantic and dull. He said 'yes' and 'no' crisply, not at all like the 'yeahs' and 'yeps' and groans I'd got from the others in his profession. All the rest of them sounded like cowboys trying to sound like Humphrey Bogart.

I prepared my speech, I told the truth, and when I was through, I waited with some patience for him to answer. The silence was lengthy.

"Are you referring to Mrs. Jhon-vieve Fisher?" He pronounced it as a pro and not as a friend.

"Yes," I replied.

"And the Woodsburys?"

"The Owen Woodsburys. Yes."

"Mrs. Holt?"

"Yes, Mr. Adams?"

"You are not by any chance trying to use me as an agent in some kind of blackmail scheme?"

That was direct enough. "No, Mr. Adams." I could out crisp a fresh saltine. "Certainly not. We are only interested in any kind of material which might pertain to my Father's well being."

"Your father's name again?"

"Colonel Warren Skinner. He has a private zoo and petting farm out on route 60. You might have heard of him." I hoped not.

Again there was silence. "No. Not that I recall, Mrs. Holt."

I sighed.

"Please believe me, Mr. Adams, we are honestly concerned. We feel there are parts of this episode that should be investigated more fully. If for no other reason than our own satisfaction. We would appreciate it if you would take the assignment, but if you feel you can't, please say so. Perhaps in that case you could suggest another agent? It's hard for us. Being so far away…" I let my voice trail away.

"I do appreciate that fact, Mrs. Holt. If you will give me until tomorrow to make a decision, I'll call you then."

He called as promised, which strengthened my belief in the man, and agreed to accept the job. We agreed on terms: one hundred and fifty dollars a day plus expenses, and parted, I thought, friends.

None of us had a clue as to what it was we were looking for. A long list of former husbands, insurance frauds, land swindles. Anything that might indicate, or prove, our suspicions were correct.

Adams agreed to call us once a week. Collect. More often if things began to hot up.

And God knows it didn't take long for that to happen.

The Bust

The next three weeks were hell. The most terrible we've lived through, and we've lived through a lot.

After the children had gone and we moved here, David and I began to find life a touch too serene, too quiet, and almost dull although neither of us is capable of boredom. We love our life. The beauty of our surroundings. The serenity. I began to collect my zoo, the horses, ponies, cats, ducks, bees, chickens, and sundries that keep me busy and content. And David set up his office workshop.

We sailed and swam and made love on the beach. We discarded our clothes and built our dream house.

I read and rode.

David sailed and invented.

But something was missing; there was no salt in our stew.

Thus the camp, which is spice enough for any curry. On the road to Hanalei the world goes by.

One day we opened our gates and the world, like the tide in a tide pool, poured in. Our land is fenced, the horses and other animals run free here, but along the highway the property is long and deep and a virgin wood, we haven't touched it, shields us from the sounds and sights of the road. We have a gate with signs on it, more to keep the animals in than the people out, which everyone soon ignored. Our first trespassers were shaggy hikers coming down from the Kalalau trail, foot-sore, dirty, and fierce-looking, searching for a safe place to spend the night.

Many of them were schoolteachers, summertime R & R, in their late twenties and early thirties. Once we had two physicists from the University of California. David and they had a ball.

They cleaned up at our house the day they left the island and it was difficult to believe they were the same two men. Shorn of their scraggy beards and tangled hair, minus a few layers of grit and sand, dressed in mufti, shoes and all, they were mundane; the most ordinary looking pair of four-eyed eggheads you can imagine.

Once we had two Irish Catholic priests from the Philippines. They helped build the irrigation system and plant our orchard. We send them lichees and red strawberry guavas when they are in season. They write and promise to return, with two little nuns next time.

I can hardly wait.

All our visitors are friends, God knows we have them by the hundreds. The world comes to us, not us to it, and sends us others from everywhere.

We are a United Nations in disguise.

Soon we were the scandal of the island, but we didn't care. We lived our own life, our way, and bothered no one. We figured if we left those scandalized, alone, they, out of courtesy, would return the compliment. We were never bored nor lonely.

*

I love to visit the camp. I am a visitor there, always welcome, but a visitor nonetheless. By now we have several permanent residents and we've become, not only friends, but good neighbors, and that's harder to do. We respect each other. We each have our territories, our space, and we don't intrude. We drop in on each other; we drop hints, which is as it should be.

"I got a'idea about them damn beetles that's been eatin' all the tomatoes. Can I see ya'bout it later?"

That would be Lew; he's our senior resident, both in age and time of residency. A tough and leathery ex-cowboy from the South West, he's a wizard with plants and animals. I couldn't hire a man to work as hard as Lew. Sometimes he makes me feel guilty. When he gets an idea it's usually a good one, and he can bring it to fruition, too. Once I offered to pay him or a job, and he wouldn't speak to me for a week.

*

I've never been to the camp and been displeased. It's a sort of family-oriented, co-educational, free-for-the-asking Bohemian Grove. People come and go and are scattered about in there like Indians in a forest.

It's always neat. It's always clean. It's always tidy. Which is more than I can say for my house and the mess outside on the road.

Compost heaps work and they don't smell.

Firepits are banked.

Territories are raked and swept, with what often turns out to be homemade brooms.

Some clever surfers from Long Beach built two elaborate two-seater out houses, what isn't hand-carved is thatched, situated in opposite corners of the forest, that even David and I like to use. One can sit inside and watch the world go by. From outside one is a contemplative Buddha, a smiling head with shoulders, bestowing benediction on the earth. Nothing like early morning ablutions in an open-air crap house, as David would say.

Sometimes there are children in the camp. Longhaired. Barefoot. Free. They are as beautiful to watch as my horses, or the birds in the trees. I have a secret spot where I like to hide and watch them at play. They've got to be the healthiest and happiest kids in the State.

There's a large community cooking and dining area usually fired-up and in use. David and I go down for dinner once in awhile, but we always take something. We never go empty handed.

Okay, I'm a romantic. Incurable. The Henry David Thoreau of the islands. But, instead of a pond and solitude, I have an entire Pacific Ocean and a camp full of people. It makes me happy.

*

On the night it happened, David and I had gone to the camp for dinner and some community entertainment. A kid from the University of Hawaii did that wonderful scene from A Thurber Carnival about the night the bed broke. He was good and we were all in stitches when it was over. Everybody went to bed laughing. We didn't wake up that way.

David and I walked home through the forest, hand-in-hand in the dark and fell asleep in each other's arms. We were routed out of bed shortly before midnight.

I awakened first; David didn't twitch. At first I thought I'd been dreaming, I do have vivid dreams, but the next crashing at the door put an end to that as an answer.

"David," I whispered, aiming my voice towards his ear, "I think there's somebody downstairs."

"Umph," he said and rolled over.

Outside a very light rain was beginning to fall. I could hear it pelting the plexi-glass bubble over our bed. No star shone through the skylight, it was a dark and a moonless night.

The crashing when it came again was louder. It shook the house. I heard a voice bellowing.

"David," I said, "there's somebody out there."

David popped into a sitting position. I pulled the covers he'd torn off me back around me.

"Shh!" he said, "Be still."

"What is it?" I whispered?

With that came a sound as though the entire lower half of the house were being torn off its foundation. We could hear voices now. We couldn't understand what they were saying. There was yet another crash.

"For Chris'sakes," David yelled, jumping out of bed, "leave the roof."

He grabbed the fur spread we used on the bed in winter, wrapped it around his waist, and headed down the stairs.

"Don't go down there like that."

"Why not? It's my house," but he dropped the spread and grabbed something out of the closet. "What the hell's going on down there?" He yelled.

I grabbed a robe, David's venerable Japanese kimono, and pattered, in my bare feet, down the after him. It was suddenly cold as hell. My feet were turning blue.

"You're under arrest," I heard a voice say.

"I'm what, you raunchy bastard?" David said and there was a thump. The scuffling and thumping sounds continued for a moment and then the lights went on.

David, half naked, seemed to be lying in the arms of an ugly snakeskin suit with boots on. Other snakeskins stood blinking on the sidelines.

Clutching David's robe around me, I burst on the scene. "You just let him go, do you hear? You just stop that!"

"Who's that?" one of the snakeskins asked.

"How in the hell do I know," another answered.

"You're under arrest."

"It's my house. You're under arrest."

"Jesus!" A snakeskin swore.

"She can't arrest me, can she?" another voice whined. "I'm the cop."

"If you're a cop, I'm Lady Godiva," I said. "Cops don't break into people's houses in the middle of the night. This is my house and I want every single one of you out of here right this minute! And you just stop pummeling my husband."

"Tell him to stop pounding on me!"

"Stop pounding on each other. My God, it's almost midnight."

"No wonder it's so damn cold. I don't have anything on under here aren't we about finished? Can't we go now?"

"Okay, men, arrest these people and get on with it."

It wasn't until the cold handcuffs snapped about my wrist that the reality of the situation hit me. We, David and I, in the privacy of our own home, were being placed under arrest. The snakeskins were cops.

"What for?" I kept repeating, but nobody would answer. "What for, David?" I repeated.

My kitchen was collapsing at my feet.

"Who's going to clean up this mess?" I cried. "What are you doing with my wheat berries?"

"What the hell's a wheat berry?"

"I don't know for cryin' out loud. Take it along to the station."

"It? They're kinda little and there's a zillion of 'em."

"Take the whole mess of'em then."

A couple of cops began kicking wheat berries, which had been scattered all over the floor, into a plastic container.

"You're stepping all over them and if you don't put the lid back on tight and drop a piece of hot ice inside, the bugs'll get in," I said.

"Sure they will lady."

"They will. How would you like to eat a piece of bread with worms in it?"

"I'd like it," the cop said. "I'd sue the bakery."

"I'm the bakery."

"So I'll sue you already."

"Fat chance. I'm going to jail."

"Take'em away," another voice commanded and the cop pushed us out the door and into the rain. When David stood up the Hopi coat he'd thrown on upstairs barely covered the essentials. He hadn't said a word.

"David, what do they want with my wheat berries?"

"Karen," David said, "why don't you shut up?"

*

We were walked, pushed, and prodded up the road through the rain. The scene at the camp was even more chaotic than the one in my kitchen. Everything seemed to have dissolved, tents were flattened. Temporary shelters were lying on their sides. People everywhere, half-clothed, not clothed at all, kids blinking and rubbing their eyes, were milling about in a circle of lights and uniformed men.

"They'll catch cold," I exclaimed. "Can't you cops- can't you men see it's raining?"

"See it?" the cop at my side grumbled. "I've been sitting in the God damn stuff for two solid hours. I'm soaked. You don't seem to care if I catch pneumonia."

"You're getting paid," I said. "They're not. At least get the children bundled up."

Several people in the camp called to me as I was escorted by. They looked cold and worried. "We're okay, Miz Holt," someone called, "Take care'a yourself, hear! We'll be okay." It sounded like Lew.

"If you'll clean up the kitchen," I yelled back, "you can cook in there 'till I get back. I've got plenty of canned goods. Hot tea'll fix you up. Give the children some cocoa. Take care of the animals."

"'Fraid not, lady. They're comin' along."

"What? Why? They haven't done anything."

"Shut up, Karen."

"That's right, Holt. Street-wise, ain't ya? Everything you say can be used against you, lady."

"My God, David, they actually say it."

With that a big Hawaiian cop pushed my cop out of the way and walked beside me to the car. He read me my rights like a father reading his half-witted kid a bedtime story. I wasn't paying attention.

"I don't see why you're arresting those poor people. Some of them just got here."

"We'll sort it out."

"I don't see why if you want to arrest people you don't do it a decent hour. What kind of cops arrest people in the middle of the might..."

I froze. My feet wouldn't move. The cop gave my arm a tug and I nearly fell on my face. "What is this?" I hissed. "Who are you? Where are you taking us?"

"All in good time. All in good time."

The road along our property line was lined with patrol cars. As we drew near, as if on signal, the blue lights began to flash and the sirens began a low-pitched whir. It was eerie and it was frightening.

David and I were shoved in the backseat of the last in a line of ten, the same car, thank God, and we pulled out.

Slowly, blue lights flashing and turning, siren softly wailing, we drove into the night.

*

At the station some kid cop gave David a pair of jockey shorts and let him make a phone call. I was left alone in the dimly lighted room, sitting on a hard concrete bench, freezing, turning blue, scared, trying to sort things out.

No one spoke to me although many people, cops and others, walked by. There seemed to be a heavy load of traffic in the cop shop that night, but no one paid any attention to me or looked me in the eye. It was as though, sitting there with my teeth chattering, my hair all hanging down, I didn't exist. I was invisible. Decent, law-abiding citizens didn't even see me. I was convinced, and I still am, that had I rolled up my eye, swallowed my tongue and fallen off the bench, they would have kept right on walking.

Long before David came back, the others arrived.

It was a mixed bag.

The people in the camp were prodded in by threes and fours, little kids, too, to sit beside me on the bench or on the concrete floor in the narrow hallway. The strays, people I'd never seen before, moved freely among us. Gaping. Watching. Rudely staring. One of these characters caught my eye and gave me a knowing wink.

No one said a word.

After a while a couple of women came in, looked around, nudged each other, whispered something I couldn't hear and started towards me. They appeared harmless. Before I had time to grasp the situation one of them whipped out a camera, with a flash, and blinded me.

I got it twice in the eyeballs.

My jaw hung slack, my hair hung lank, and startled by the flash, I'd released the front of David's kimono. I gaped revealingly.

The only reason I didn't make the front page is because David looked so much cuter in his borrowed shorts.

Dozens of pictures were taken that night. I've kept none for my scrapbook.

After the picture taking session the camp people became restless. At one point I tried counting noses, but that was impossible, people moved about too much. Everything was in flux. There was constant churning.

And murmuring.

We were a peaceful bunch. I think everyone was in shock.

I was startled to discover Kuuipo, Bobby Lim, the Postmaster, in the crowd. He was standing in a corner speaking to a big Portuguese cop. They were talking together earnestly. Kuuipo was wearing a brown-leather jacket and white cotton boxer shorts with over-size cinnamon-red ants running rampant across the front and back. He was shaking his head violently.

I'd never seen him in a pair of shorts before. He was a stocky little guy; the muscles in his calves bulged. Except for the violent head movement, he seemed undisturbed.

In the middle of the room the seven members of the skiing team held conference. They spoke quietly but with great animation. Poor things. They thought they'd found a safe haven. When this was over I must try to call their parents or their coach.

At least they were clothed. They'd been sleeping in what looked like red, white, and blue kid's pajamas, minus the feet. Even sleeping they were a team.

I recognized three kids from the church camp next door. They looked bewildered but plucky. I wondered if any of our neighbors, the church members, had witnessed our departure. If they had, help might be on the way.

One curious sight, as curious because I recognized them, as that they were there, I was decidedly a-political, were two members of the City Council and the Mayor. I couldn't bring myself to believe they'd been sleeping in the camp. If they had, they were the only ones with sense, or time, to put their clothes on. The Mayor even wore a coat and tie.

Two prim and proper elementary school teachers, who had arrived yesterday from California, looked anything but prim and proper. Of the entire bunch, these two young women easily answered the description of 'hippy'.

Minus their granny glasses, walking shorts, and sturdy shoes, long hair hanging down and T-shirts, wet from the rain, they could have escaped from any one of a dozen X-rated movies.

The rest of the crowd was made up of surfers, boys and girls, some from the mainland, some local. Most of them looked bored. One brawny kid had actually gone to sleep on the cold cement floor.

I envied him.

Most of the kids were wrapped in towels or paisley spreads. One kid was a knockout in a bright yellow sheet tied over one shoulder like a toga. This kid had a long red beard and thick curly hair. His eyes were fierce and blue. If he started to sing, I'd know for sure I was in the wrong dream.

Not one of us, except the Mayor and his gang, had the good sense to grab a pair of shoes. We were, all of us, mud halfway up our calves. The hem of my robe was a solid band of thick red slime.

We were a sight.

When David appeared out of an office behind the counter, a cheer went up. David raised his hand and there was silence. "I called Ty. He'll be here first thing in the morning. He says for all of us to keep our cool. Obey the," he paused "our captors and keep your mouths shut. He'll have us out of here before noon tomorrow."

Another cheer.

"That's enough of that," a cop said. I watched the little fat Mayor sidle edgewise toward the door.

Everyone knew who Ty was, and he is a big contributor to politicos. The Mayor had suddenly decided to uninvolve himself.

"We'll need fingerprints and pictures so form two lines. The cameras here," the cop pointed, "the blotter's there. Give the officer your name and age and when that's done form another line at the door. We'll take it from there."

No one cheered.

I rose from my bench, holding my robe closed, and walked over to meet David as he walked out from behind the counter. I spoke to the skiers as I passed, "Take cheer, girls. You had no part in whatever is going on. Look at it this way, you've had an adventure you can one day tell your grandchildren about."

"That's it exactly, Mrs. Holt," the leader of the team replied. "That's what I told them. It's an adventure. We'll be okay. You take care of yourself and don't be upset about us."

I nodded.

"Ladies," I said to the schoolteachers. "I'm really sorry about this…"

"Goddam pigs!" the littlest schoolteacher said and her eye glinted sparks.

"We were in Berkeley during the riots," the other teacher quickly explained. "Lori and I were maced. We spent eighteen hours in Santa Rita prison."

"Filthy pigs."

"I'm sure this won't be anything like that," I said. "Our cops are good guys. Honest."

"They're all pigs."

I walked on.

"Bobby," under the circumstances I was afraid to call him by his endearment, Kuuipo means 'darling', "what are you doing here?"

"Moose and me were having a rap session after the show. Finally crashed and then these guys," he jerked his head towards a cop, "busted in."

"Yes. They did do that."

"They say I don't have to get busted with you guys but nothing they can do can stop me. If you guys go to the pokey I'm going to the pokey. These guys," again he glared at the big cop, "are crazy man! Looney. Lolo."

"Hush, Bobby, don't make it worse. Thanks for being a staunch friend."

"Staunch," he grinned. "I got ants in my pants." He did a little jig.

I giggled.

"Remember what Ty said," David hollered across the room, "en la boca serrade entra la mosca."

"Ants," Bobby said. "Ants in my pants." He did another jig.

"What's this all about anyway?" I asked David when I reached his side. "Why were we hauled down there? What were we arrested for?"

"Possession. Seven pounds of primo buds. Grass. Pakalolo. Weed. Marijuana. Mary Jane. Packaged neat and tidy and sealed in seal-a-meal Baggies and hidden everywhere. It's a drug rap."

"That's ridiculous," I said. David didn't say anything. He steered me into line.

Ty Blue

They separated us for the short ride back to Wailua. The men rode in one long checkered cab the women in another. It took several trips to transport all of us.

I was in the first cab. As I lined up with the others preparing to board, one of the surfers waiting in line for the other cab yelled, "It's off to the Hilton, kiddies. Dirty sheets and the lice can jump six feet."

"Bugs," one of the girls shuddered. "I hate bugs. If I even see a bug I'll scream."

"Ah, don't lis'sen to'em, kid. He's been in too many Mexican jails," a cop said. "There's no bugs an' the sheets are clean. Food's not so bad, too. My wife does lots a' the cooking."

Sheets, as it turned out, clean or otherwise, were not to be the problem. By the time we all got to jail the sun was up, the birds were singing, and golfers, on the public golf course across the highway, were already out hitting a few.

It was ladies last at the unloading, a slight those of us in the cab felt not at all. The old green prison was shabby, disreputable-looking structure. The paint was peeling and dirty. There were thick rusty bars at the doors and windows and many of the panes of glass behind the bars were missing, cracked or broken. It was a drafty old hoosegow.

We watched through the windows in the back of the cab, as the men were marched single-file up the steps and into the building. They were a ragged-looking crew. I felt bad about their muddy feet. From inside we could hear the sound of heavy doors slamming shut.

"Now I know why they call it the slammer," somebody said, but nobody laughed. When it was our turn we were hustled out of the cab, across a patchy strip of dying grass, and into a small, filthy reception room on the first floor. Directly in front of us was a wall of heavy steel bars behind which the men were locked. We could see a row of cells lined against the back wall of the building. No one was in those cells. The doors were open. Several young men in other cells clutched the bars and stared out at us. I didn't see David.

"It's okay, girls," one of the guys said, "we'll be right here if you need us."

One of the girls giggled.

From the entrance room we hurried up a narrow flight of stairs. At the top of the stairs was an immense barn of a room; it ran the entire length of the building. Instead of cells, iron beds lined the back wall. Along the far wall were three open toilets and several cracked and rusted basins. The bars in the women's windows didn't seem as formidable as the bars in the men's cells downstairs. We were the weaker sex after all. Then I remembered those husky skiers. Not to worry, sergeant, I thought, if the bars on our prison had been made of silly putty you'd never catch a member of our team breaking out. Those girls would sit on their bunks with their hands primly folded until hell froze over if someone in authority told them to.

I loved them for that.

As for that pair of schoolteachers, I'd not have been a bit surprised if they had hacksaws hidden about their person. If they wanted out, petite and fragile as the darling creatures appeared, they'd have got out. If I was a National Guardsman, and I caught sight of that pair, I'd get the hell out of their way. Fast.

And I loved them for that.

We heard the cabs start up on the way back to town to pick up the others. I walked to the barred windows and peered out, just to see what it felt like. What a pretty morning. The sun was beginning to pop above the trees on the palm-strewn golf course and the ocean was as blue as the early morning sky. There was no dividing line at the horizon. I felt sorry for all those free-swinging golfers out there in the open air; they were out there all alone.

We were together. In the slammer. Finger-printed. Arrested. Mugged.   Criminals all of us.

They were quite a number of us gathered at the windows now. When the next cab load arrived all of us cheered. Downstairs somebody started to sing; we'd lost Jake, but not Old Black Joe. As the rest of the girls filed up the stairs, we all joined in.

When Ty arrived, natty in his blue-dyed boots and blue polo shirt, the Wailua Hilton was rocking. Just after Ty arrived two yellow church buses drove up. The clan was gathering.

The schoolteachers and the skiers were practicing a bumpy hula in the middle of the room and everyone not dancing was hanging on the bars singing.

We were so noisy the lonely golfers across the highway paused to listen.

Ty looked up and waved. I couldn't tell whether the expression on his face was a grin or a grimace, but either way it didn't dull my spirits one bit. I kept right on singing, "I wanna go back to my little grass shack in Kealakekua Hawaii."

*

Ty had arranged bail for all of us, put up the money himself, and even arranged transportation for the whole gang of us to get home; he'd been at the police station when the minister of the church called about his boys. Somebody had seen us. Everyone needs a lawyer like Ty Blue and friends like our neighbors.

David, Ty, the minister, who was driving, and all the girls and I rode home in one of the big yellow buses marked First Church of God and the Holy Ghost Beach Camp in bright red letters.

We were subdued.

Ty told us from outside it hadn't sounded like singing, it sounded as though a riot were in progress. It wasn't until we got to Kilauea that I remembered Father. Shows you, doesn't it? Six days ago the most terrible thing that ever happened to me, in a long time, anyway, was my Father's forthcoming marriage. Driving home from jail in David's muddy kimono, with all the kids, David and the minister, it was hard to understand what the fuss had been about. It was so remote from my present condition it might as well never have happened. All that poor man wanted to was to get laid. How could I have been so mean? When Adams got in touch with us next time I'd call the whole thing off.

After last night I wondered if anything could ever upset me again.

It wasn't long before I got the answer to that, and I didn't consult the I Ching.

*

Holt Camp, as we drove up the drive, was a disaster area. It looked as though it had been turned inside out and upside down. The girls in the back of the bus groaned.

"The horses!" I cried. "My god, David, the horses." I didn't wait for the bus to stop but jumped out, kimono flying and raced barefoot through the trees.

The barn hadn't been touched. It looked exactly as it had when I left it last night. As far as I could see I had a barn full of bored, hungry horses. Nothing more.

I ran down the covered passageway opening stall doors. It was so late, nearly two o'clock, I thought it wiser to let them wait until dinner to eat. They could graze. None of them would fall down faint from starvation. Their water buckets were full, so they'd not run out of that, which was a relief. I felt better already. Some of the girls who'd followed me were fussing over the horses, patting them, talking to them, the horses seemed willing to forgive, but we could hear cries of dismay and anger coming from the camp.

David, Ty, and the minister had driven to the house, followed by a pack of bounding, barking dogs. The cats were not in sight, but when I opened the stall door, chickens and ducks appeared out of nowhere to peck around the rich nut-smelling bedding.

"Where shall we begin, Mrs. Holt?" one of the girls, the littlest schoolteacher, asked.

"We'll begin by taking a swim," I said. "I feel grungy as hell. Bet you do, too. Call the others."

Before we could gather the others, David, Ty, and the minister came running from the house.

"Don't touch anything," David said. "Get a camera someone. Who has a camera? We have to get pictures of this."

"Why? What is it, David? The horses are fine."

"It's incredible that's what it is," the minister said, "if I hadn't seen it with my own eye I would never have believed the police could be so destructive."

"My shop was demolished," David said, "thousands of dollars worth of damage. You won't believe the house."

"I'll tell you what I don't believe," Ty said. "I don't think believe the police did this. Someone get a photographer out here."

"One of our members is a professional photographer. I'll call him. He'll be glad to help. He can also act as a witness. He's a respected man in the community. He won't believe this either. Meanwhile if you folks need anything, food, clothing, showers, baths, help yourselves to our facilities." The minister ran back to his van and drove away.

"I don't know what the hell to make of this," David said.

"Run down and tell those kids not to touch anything," I said to the schoolteacher. "Please." My knees were weak. Why had they spared the barn? The horses, locked in their stalls, had been sitting ducks. I sank into a canvas chair.

David stood with his feet planted apart, his arms folded, looking past the barn out to sea. "I haven't the guts to check the boat."

"There was malicious destruction done here," Ty said. "We'll get pictures. Then we'll talk. I'm glad I got to see this with my own eyes."

When the phone ran I reached for it with a despairing hand. "Hello," I said.

"Karen, pet. How are you this fine day?"

"Fine. Is that you?" He'd forgotten to reverse the charges. Well, something good had to happen.

"We're having a terrible time here, Karen," he said.

I groaned. "Are you?"

"All of you are fine I trust?"

"Fine. Just fine." David shook his head at me and Ty put his finger to his lips. "What seems to be the trouble?"

I listened to his troubles for what seemed hours. It was not necessary to reply. At last he took a breath.

"I'll ask. I certainly will. As far as the other is concerned, send me a picture. Then I'll have a better idea. After all I don't know what the lady looks like."

He seemed satisfied, said good-bye and hung up.

"He wants to know if you'll be best man, David."

"Sure. They can get married in the vestibule of the jail."

"And he wants to know what color the bride should wear."

"Black and white. Black and white stripes."

"No. Everyone else'll be wearing striped. Tie-dye. We'll dip her in Easter egg dye and tell everyone Hugh Hefner sent her."

"Very funny, Karen," David said.

"I'm not splitting a gut. Let's get you kids cleaned up and get on with this," Ty said.

*

We cleaned up at the church camp, and, after we fed and put the animals to bed, Ty, David, and I drove to Lorraine's for dinner.

The church people fed our guys and put them up for the night; by the time we'd finished photographing everything it was after dark. We'd cleared a place for Ty to sleep, and David and I, too. Whoever they were they had let the water out of the waterbed. The wall-to-wall carpeting in our bedroom would have to be taken out. The planks of cedar on the ceiling below were stained. We'd be lucky if we didn't have to replace the one and refinish the other.

"Now remember," Ty said, 'nothing about this at dinner. We'll talk when we get home."

It was a glum and gloomy dinner. Lorraine clucked around us like a fretful old hen and gave us double portions of everything, but it didn't help.

We drove home in silence.

Before we want to bed, Ty made David and me walk through the scene. He wanted to know everything.

What had awakened us? Sounds? Lights? Voices?

Did David walk downstairs in the dark? How come? Did I? When did the lights go on? Before or after the scuffle? Who turned them on? Were they just the lights in the kitchen or did the entire house light up? The upstairs? Was it dark?

How many men were in the house when we first saw them? Well, about how many? Did more enter when the lights went out? How many? How many men were in the house when we left? Were they all wearing the same type of clothing? Why did I insist on calling them snakeskins?

Did we see anyone go upstairs?

About what time was it?

After he'd drained us dry he went to the camp. He made David and me stay in the house.

I got busy cleaning up the kitchen and tried not to cry. My lovely oiled-teak floor was a battlefield of pits and craters. It looked as though someone had run over it with a sheep's foot.

"Do you think we can sand it smooth again, David?"

"We'll leave it. Battle scars belong."

"In the kitchen?"

"In the kitchen."

"What's going on, David?" I asked for the fifth time.

"I wish I knew, Karen. I wish to hell I knew."

Long before Ty came back we were fast asleep.

*

Before Ty flew back to Honolulu, he had a private talk with David. I was not asked to participate. But when Ty kissed me good-bye, he said, "You'll be fine, Karen. Just remember that. You'll both, all of you, will be fine. That's a nice bunch down there," he nodded towards the camp. "They'll make good witnesses. You've got good things going for you, too, don't forget that. Now give us a big hug. I'll be back for the arraignment."

Lorraine, a couple of her friends, a witness from the New Papeete, all the girls from the camp, some of the ladies from the church, and I got busy in the house. I cried only once and that was when I found I had to toss out shards of a pottery cat my youngest daughter had made me when she was in the first grade.

When David came back the house was neated up, looked cozy, in fact, and good smells were pouring out of the kitchen.

"Okay, David, what did he say?"

"Not to worry," David said.

'No. Really. I'm a big girl, I can take it."

"Nothing bad. Or that secretive. Just complicated, that's all."

"Complicated? How?"

"Lots of people involved for one thing. There's a lot more here than meets the eye, Karen."

"I'm involved here, David."

"You don't want to know."

"Do too."

He tried to smile. "Well there's good news and there's bad news."

"First the good news?"

He nodded. "I'm clean for one thing. I have a perfect record. I don't even get parking tickets."

"True. Go on."

"That's it."

"Long list."

"Wait'll you hear the bad news."

"I can barely."

He sighed. "You. You haven't a perfect record. You have a dossier that would choke a horse."

"My war years catching up with me?" I grinned. "I made the enemy's list." I patted myself on the back.

"Not funny, Karen."

"Go on. I can live being the Jane Fonda of the Pacific."

"Maybe you better sit down."

I sat.

"Ty thinks it's a frame up."

"I know it's a frame up. But who'd want to frame us?"

"The state."

"The state? You mean they're that mad at me?" I grinned again.

"Don't get the big head, kid. It isn't you. It's the land. There's talk in Honolulu of condemning this land. Anyway," David sighed, "that's all he's got going."

"Condemning our land! For what?

"For a park."

"They can do that any time they want. Why the hanky-panky?"

"This is just speculation, Karen. Ty believes us. It's got to be a frame. But who? Why? The land is the only thing he's got going. He figures if they can prove they're condemning a filthy hipped up drug scene it'll look better all the way around."

"Keeps the good citizen in line, eh? If he keeps his nose clean his land won't be condemned."

David nodded. "Something like that. And there's always the question of money."

"They'd rather steal it?"

"They'd rather steal it."

"Is that all?"

"No. It gets worse."

"Jesus!"

"The media."

This time I nodded, remembering the woman with the flash.

"According to the radio we're the Manson family of Kauai. They're having a field day. I'm a mad scientist. You're a kook. We're growers. Addicts. Pushers."

"Baby boilers."

"Yep."

"Can't we sue?"

"They're careful to leave themselves an out. It's all inference at this point."

"Go on."

"I made the front page in the morning paper."

"In your cute little shorts?"

"We even made the Editorial page. Slow day in the islands. You made the inside page, Ma, sorry. Maybe next time."

When the phone rang, I jumped three feet. It was long distance. Collect. Before I could tell him we'd changed our minds, he began, "I don't have much, Mrs. Holt. But it's all there. It's coming through. Can you give me more time?"

"Of course," I sighed.

"If I double the manpower I can move faster. Are you in a rush?"

"How long the way you're going?"

"Maybe a week. Maybe more. Maybe less."

"That says it. Do what you have to do, Mr. Adams. Call again. Next week. Or sooner if you get something juicy. And thank you. We really appreciate what you're doing."

He hung up.

David sighed. "The old man?"

"Yes, my daddy's bride-to-be is really Count Dracula in drag."

"It never rains," David said.

"Can you believe those bastards punched holes in the waterbed?"

Armed Rape

It took all of us, with outside help, two days to restore order. We spent the third day repairing what we could. Insurance men stumbled in and out shaking their heads. A team of carpet cleaners flew in from Honolulu and removed the bedroom carpet. It would have to be flown back to Oahu, where, they shook their heads, they would do their best.

We were filling the new waterbed. David and I would christen it this evening.

We had to order glass from the mainland to fit the huge living room window, so we carefully removed broken pieces and taped and tacked clear plastic sheets in place. The diffused light did strange things to my beautiful room; it was like walking around on the bottom of a dirty fish bowl.

It had been a discouraging business. Over and over we were reminded that nothing would ever be quite the same again.

The elegant outhouse at the camp was nothing. Kindling.

My lovely tapa pillows were nothing. Rags.

Later in the afternoon someone smuggled in a three-day stack of newspapers. City and local. It was like Christmas for the kids, the first good laugh they'd had since we left the Hilton. I tried not to look, but that was impossible.

David, glaring out of a murky 5x5 front page shot, looked like a pale-faced Kung Fu killer minus his droopy drawers.

There was an entire pictorial section in the Sun devoted to the camp. THIS IS HOW THEY LIVED was the head that screamed across the page. All of the pictures, of course, had been taken after the destruction. It looked like the city dump on a busy day.

The editorials David told me about warned concerned citizens to beware outside groups eroding island morals. The editorial in the local paper began, "Where does island hospitality end and the preservation of our true Hawaii life-style begin?"

"The dangers of sick mainland cults invading our easy-going island people are profound," said another.

They both ended on a pious note, asking concerned citizens to carefully differentiate between troublemakers and the real HVB tourist.

"The real HVB tourist is fat and ugly. He spends the money."

"He's seventy years old and drives a red Datsun rent-a-car. Look out for him. He won't pick you up hitching, he'll run you down."

"He'll pick us up," piped a cute little blonde. "And if big fat mama wasn't in the front seat with him we'd have to beat him off with a stick."

"You're missing it," drawled a tall slender girl, "the real HVB tourists is three haoles in glow-in-the-dark muu muus. I don't know what's worse, their saggy old arms or those atrociously phony Hawaiian prints."

"I like the old guys that wear black silk socks with garters and sandals"

"I like the ones who find something to bitch about so they won't have to leave a tip."

"How about the ones who live on soda crackers they steal at Woolworth's?"

I decided it was time to break this up. "Kids you sound awful. Someday you're going to get old and fat."

"I will not get fat," the little blonde said.

"You didn't get old and fat, Mrs. Holt," said the slender girl.

I was indignant. "Well, I'm not a hundred years old either."

"Neither are they. Ninety percent of those slovenly old bats are not any older than you," the tall girl answered.

"Someday you will learn," I said, "that people age differently. But whether I'm old or fat is not the point. The point is it's ugly for young people to say such cruel things about older people. If anything you should pity them and be kind to them. Weren't you taught to respect your elders?"

The tall girl looked down her nose at me and said, as she strode off, "When my elders do something I can respect them for I'll respect them."

She had me there.

The kids continued to have fun picking on the tourist. It's true, I'm afraid; we seem to be getting a sadder and shabbier lot every year. I continued reading. One rather notoriously oddball columnist picked up on David's inventions, quoting, he said, a close friend, "David Holt…the mad genius…is at home with his sinister mechanical tricks as he is with his somewhat weird assumption that the universe is shaped like a three-cornered hat…"

This guy was a three-dot man.

I didn't think I would say anything about that to David.

I, he continued, on the other hand, was an outspoken pagan more at home in a Bullfinch than the Good Book. "Karen calls herself a born again Druid...the last of the practicing Luddites...she and Holt make an unlikely pair.

"She's a kook who loves her horses more than her children...and it shows. A long-haired middle-age hippy with revolutionary overtones...if she dislikes this country so much why doesn't she move to Russia?"

That guy read my war record, anyway. I hope it was juicy.

My picture, the same in both papers, appeared on page six in one, and on the back page of the other. It should have appeared in the X-rated theater section. I looked too dumb to be a rebellious anything, but I sure as god looked my age. A little more Juke than Kallikak, perhaps, but if I were a hip anything, it was hippy retard from a cathouse in the Ozarks.

I looked as though I ate horses.

Fortunately, not even one of my own children would have recognized me.

When David came home that night from a terrible day in his neck of the woods, I was still steaming.

"I'll middle age revolutionary him," I snapped.

"What, Karen?"

"Those damn reporters make me mad."

"I told you not to read the papers."

"How could I not read them? They were blowing in the wind."

"You shouldn't have brought them here."

"I didn't."

"Who did?" David snapped.

"How in the hell do I know? The kids had stacks of them."

"Damn them. Damn the whole bunch of them. And you, too."

"I beg your pardon."

"If it hadn't been for you and all those kooks you collect…"

"Kooks…"

"Yes, kooks! You collect them. And I'm damn well fed up with them. If it hadn't been because of them, none of this would have happened."

I sniffed. "That's absurd."

"Is it? Think about it. You should see my shop."

"All you think about is your damn shop. Take a look at my house." I shouted.

"What the hell do I care about your house?"

"You live here, too."

"Don't I know it."

"Well, if you don't like it there's the door."

He used it and slammed it behind him.

I took dinner out of the oven and put it in the refrigerator, turned off the lights, walked upstairs and went to bed. The waterbed had not filled.

The damn bare floor was cold.

*

I didn't sleep well. I never do when David's not beside me, but I was too worn out to stay awake and brood. It must have been close to one o'clock in the morning when I awoke. I felt around in the bed for David and then remembered, I was sleeping on the floor and David was sleeping elsewhere. My feelings were still hurt. I was still mad, but not at David.

The moon was full and shining gloriously through the bubble skylight in the roof; it did nothing to brighten up my spirits. I thrashed around in the void and tangled myself in the sheets. It was a good thing David hadn't spent the night, we'd be black and blue. I pulled the covers this way, pushed them that way, pounded a pillow, tossed and turned. It was hopeless. I'd never get back to sleep.

"Oh the hell with it," I said to the moon and got up. I put on a nice velour robe, and a pair of thick furry slippers, and walked downstairs in the dark.

The living room was gloomy with filtered moonlight. I peered through the shadows. I couldn't see anything, but I could feel the emptiness; David wasn't here.

I remembered I hadn't eaten and was beginning to wonder how cold eggplant Parmesan would taste. Better, the longer I thought about it. When a shattering shriek filled the night I swung around so fast I banged my elbow on the counter. "Damn it," I swore.

"Help! Help me," the voice, a woman's voice, screamed again.

I didn't think. I ran. I lost one slipper and stubbed my toe, cursed again, and ran out of the kitchen door and down the steps. The forest was in deep shadow but the beach was brilliant in the moonlight. I ran towards it.

"No! No! No!" The woman screamed again.

"I'm coming!" I yelled.

"I'm coming," I heard David yell and then I heard the shot.

When I got to the beach I saw them in the moonlight. David, in a pair of shorts, was standing over a body fallen to the ground. I could see the glint of a gun barrel in his hand. It was smoking.

"David!" I screamed.

"Karen!" He yelled back.

I ran towards him.

"Rape!" screamed the body on the beach and began to writhe. It, she, was naked. "Help!"

I reached David's side at the same time the light appeared in the forest. "Stop in the name of the law!" A voice called. With that the girl on the beach rose to her knees, it looked as though she were having a difficult time getting out from between David's legs.

"Officer! He raped me!" The girl flung herself at the cop.

"David," I hissed.

"They! They raped me," the girl screamed.

"Okay, girlie, it's okay now. You there! You two! Don't move."

"They're filthy rotten perverts. They…"

"Okay," the cop said trying to disentangle himself from the clutching girl.

"There were two of them officer," David yelled waving the smoking revolver, "they ran down the beach. If we hurry we can catch them. They can't get far." He started to move.

"Don't move," the cop yelled.

"Liar!" The girl screamed. "Don't believe him. Don't leave me alone with them."

"Quiet down," the cop shouted. "Drop that gun! Drop it. Now!"

David dropped the gun.

"Officer the young lady's hysterical."

"Ain't she though," the cop said.

"I'm David Holt. This," he turned to me, "is my wife Karen."

"La de da," the cop said, "and I'm Charlie Chan."

"We came in answer to this young woman's calls for help."

"And I'm the Japanese Sand Man. I could hear you two perverts yellin'.

The girl had dropped to the sand and lay sobbing at the cop's feet. He took off his jacket and threw it to her. "Girl," he ordered, "I want you to get up and run to the house. When you get there I want you to turn on the lights. Now! Go!" She went.

"You two stand where you are. Don't move a muscle. I can shoot this thing. Maybe I don't want to, maybe I do, but you give me one little excuse and I promise you I will."

Just as the lights went on in the house, we heard the sound of voices approaching from the camp.

"Holt," the cop ordered again, "If those are your guys you better get them to stop where they are."

I could see the muzzle of the gun pointed right at us.

"Whoever's out there," David yelled, "Stop! Stay right where you are. Everything's under control."

"Are you okay, Mrs. Holt?"

"I'm fine. Go back to bed."

"Officer," David said when he heard the footsteps move away, "whatever you think this is, it isn't. My wife had nothing to do with it in any case. Let her go. She can be of help to that poor girl."

"Your wife stays where she is." The cop shouted, never taking his eyes off us. "You in the house. Get to the phone. Call the police. Tell them who and where you are. You two come with me. Don't talk. And don't get any funny ideas." He motioned us ahead of him with his gun and followed us through the forest.

For the second time in less than a week, we were handcuffed and pushed into patrol cars.

Only this time David rode in one car, I rode in another.

*

Of all the nights I've lived through, that had to be the worst. The cops were horrid to me. I thought how badly I'd felt the last time being ignored, and wished I could receive the same treatment now.

I was dragged out of the car and shoved up the walk into the police station. I lost my other slipper and was not allowed to retrieve it. The cop taking my fingerprints and the cop taking my picture were mean, sullen, and ugly. To them I was the vilest of all living creatures, a pervert, a child molester, an abuser.

David and I were kept separated. If the cops had had their way, or the station had been bigger, we'd have not been allowed a glimpse of each other. Once I saw him being pushed out a door in a corner of the room. I hoped that meant he'd made his phone call. He looked as grim and mean as the cops.

I was taken to Wailua first. The stairs were steeper and narrower than I recalled. The painted walls were filthier. The steel door when it slammed shut sounded formidable, not funny, and certainly not flimsy.

One bare light hung from the ceiling on a frayed black cord. It must have been all of twenty-five watts. The beds were empty, but I couldn't bear to lie down on one. I pulled a straight wooden chair out from against the wall and into the center of the room, beneath the bulb, and there I sat, prepared to spend the night. Even though I was sure no one was in the room with me, the shadows in the corners and under the beds were threatening. I didn't hear David come in, if he came in. I wasn't sure he'd been brought here. I was alone. I heard no sound. No voice. No footsteps. There was no one in the entire world but me, and I sat behind bars on a hard chair, under a cold light, in a bare, empty room.

I sobbed. Prettily. No blubbers. No bawls nor bleats. No drippy red nose. Why make a scene? There was no one there to see.

Daylight began to filter through the windows casting long-barred shadows across the floor. When they reached the chair, the overhead light went out.

Below I could hear the first faint sounds of morning. Whoever was moving around downstairs was being quiet. I heard a door creak open. I thought I heard another door open and then close, water running, a toilet being flushed. I thought of the open toilets in the back of the room and felt sick. I'd die before I'd use one of them.

Outside, a car pulled off the highway and into the courtyard. It sounded as though it stopped directly under my window. Whoever it was had driven right to the door. I could hear him, or her, whistling. A happy tune. There was the sound of low conversation in the room below. Footsteps started up the stairs. I rose from my seat and walked to the windows, turning my back to the iron door and whoever might appear outside.

"Mornin' Mary Sunshine," a cheery voice called. "Can't you two stay out of trouble long enough for me to get one night's sleep?"

"Ty," I turned and ran to the barred door. I reached through the bars to touch him. The hand that clasped mine was warm and comforting.

Ty stood there smiling like the bluebird of happiness, but there was a different look in his eyes. He put his finger to his lips. "You look a sight, Karen," he opened the hand he held and something was in it. It was a small slip of paper. I clutched it for all it was worth.

Ty started back down the stairs whistling again. "David and I are going to have to have a talk about this universe business," he called back over his shoulder. "I always thought it was shaped like a banana."

I laughed in spite of myself.

I walked over to a basin and with my back to the iron bars read the note. It said, "Don't say ONE word! Keep your pretty mouth shut. See you soon. Ty." I tore up the note, considered eating it, and then decided to flush it down the john. I walked over to one of the beds and crawled in. The next thing I knew the steel door to my prison was being opened and Ty was saying, "Sleeping like a baby. Well come on, baby, let's get you out of here and home to your own little bed."

I yawned, stretched, and walked to the door, down the steps and into the sunshine. David was nowhere in sight.

"Where's David?"

Ty put his hand and my shoulder, shot me a perfectly vile look, and jerked his head towards the car. I shut up and got in. I didn't say another word until we were well outside town.

"All right, Ty, surely this car isn't bugged."

He laughed. A real laugh for a change.

"What's going on?" I asked him

"I wish to hell I knew. I really do."

"Is David out?"

"No."

I thought about that. "How come I got out?"

"Because I threatened to close their whole jail house down if they didn't let you go," he replied. "I've threatened to close that place down before, but this time I meant it. You could have been locked in that room with anyone. A nut. A murderer. A crazy drunk. It's a disgrace."

I shivered. To take my mind off what might have been, he made me tell him everything I remembered from the night before.

"Are you sure you left nothing out?"

"No. Nothing."

"David was not with you?"

"No."

"Where was he?"

"I don't know."

"Does he sleep somewhere other than in your bed often?"

I giggled. "No. Oh, once in a great while if he has a really heavy project going he'll stay late in the office. But I can't remember the last time he didn't sleep in my bed. Oh, " I remembered, "yes, I can. He went to San Francisco on business for a couple of days last summer."

"Rape anybody?"

I laughed.

"You didn't go?"

I shook my head.

"Why not?"

"I had a sick horse."

He nodded. "Okay. So all you know is that when you got to the beach David was there lying on top of some woman."

"Certainly not," I was indignant. I didn't say that at all. "He was standing. He even had his shorts on. I didn't know it was a woman, a girl, whatever, until later."

"You didn't know it was a woman?"

"No. Not then. It was just a body. I couldn't determine the sex. I thought he'd shot someone."

Ty swore. "Why did you think he'd shot someone?"

"Because. I told you this already," I looked at him, "because I heard the shot and the gun was shining in the moonlight."

"What gun?"

"The gun I told you about. The cops took it." What was the matter with Ty? Hadn't he even been listening? "The gun he was holding in his hand. It was smoking."

"They won't have far to look for the smoking gun anyway," he sighed.

"Is there such a thing as armed rape?"

Ty laughed. "Good girl. I like you better when you're being funny."

"Me, too. It's your turn. Say something funny."

"You didn't associate the scream you heard with the women, the figure, on the beach?"

"That's funny? No. I didn't associate the scream with the body on the beach. I thought the body was dead. Dead bodies don't scream."

"You're going to make a wonderful witness. For them. When did you decide it was a woman?"

"When the cop arrived. She jumped up and ran. She screamed that 'he' was trying to rape her and then when she saw me she screamed 'they' were trying to rape her. Did rape her. Oh, what a mess."

"You said 'trying'."

"Yes, but I'm pretty sure she said we did. They did."

"She said 'they'?"

"I'm pretty sure she said 'they'."

"The cop said he heard you and David screaming obscenities. Having orgiastic fits."

"Doing what?" And then I began to laugh. I laughed until I cried, and I cried for real. Blubbers, red nose, hiccups, bawls and bleats. Ty was immune. "Are you over your hysterics?"

"Yes," I hiccupped.

"What was so funny?"

I told him and he laughed, too. "'I'm coming David' is hardly obscene. The cops in these parts must certainly have delicate ears."

"Is everything going to be all right?"

He sucked his teeth. "Oh," he said, "I hope so."

"You hope so?"

"Well, frankly, it's a fiasco."

"But you believe us?"

"Of course I believe you. I wouldn't be here if I didn't. I believe that guilty parties ought to cool their heels in the cooler for a few days. Makes 'em more tractable."

Tears came to my eyes. "You must have been up all night."

"Since four," he yawned. "David called about four. I left the house, caught the red-eye, and got here about six-thirty. I've been fighting with that damn judge ever since. If it'll make you happier I got him out of bed, too."

"Bet that made him happy. Can you get David out?"

"Of bed?"

I didn't laugh.

"With your help," he said.

"Name it."

"Money. Lots of it. The bail will probably be set between fifty and sixty thou. There's a lot of flak about the case."

"Can do."

"Good girl," he said.

He drove me to the house, dropped me off, and I pointed to the furry slipper I'd lost on the porch the night before. " I lost the other one at the police station."

"Okay, Cinderella, meet me at Henry's at noon. Bring money. I'll buy lunch. Then we'll go rescue Prince Charming. I got the pumpkin," he slapped his hand against the side of the car."

"Should I bring some clothes?"

"That's what I like," he said as he drove away, "positive thinking."

"I'll bring some clothes."

*

I explained to a delegation of worried people from the camp that everything was okay; we'd tell all later, and then I got busy. It was quite a morning, but when I met Ty again, promptly at noon. I had the money. Cash. He bought lunch. We ate pastrami on rye with pickles and beer. Afterwards we drove to the police station; again I was warned to say nothing. "Never talk in a police station," Ty said. We paid David's bail: it was only twenty thousand, good old Ty got a receipt for the money and drove out to Wailua to pick up David. After we freed him we stopped at the bank to return the rest of the cash to my account.

"I get nervous hauling around that kind of money," I said.

"Me, too," Ty said. "Now, Karen, I don't want you to say anything. Let David talk."

And David told his story.

He'd been sleeping at his office, and he, too, had been awakened by the bright moonlight. Like me, he was no longer mad. Also, like me, he was hungry.

He started towards the house, naked as usual, when he saw three figures on the beach. They were acting strangely, David said he couldn't tell what they were up to, but it didn't look right to him, so he turned around and went back to his office and put his shorts on.

"You walked up the beach?"

"No," David replied, "I walked in the shadows of the trees, but when the girl started to scream I ran out on the beach."

"Were there lights on at the house?"

"I didn't notice if there were. Once the girl really started screaming I just ran." Like me, he didn't stop to think.

"What happened then?"

"One of the figures fell to the beach. The other two took off running."

"Away from you?"

"Yes."

"Can you describe them?"

"No. Not really. One of them had long hair. I could see that, but they were too far away to see much else and running fast."

He'd almost reached the girl's side when he heard me swear and the door bang. He was afraid someone was after me. When he heard me yell, he yelled back. That's what the cop heard, and that's when David took a shot at the fleeting shadows.

"It was a stupid thing to do it only made them run faster. They were too far away to hit. But at times like those you're not always thinking straight."

Ty grunted.

I told David about the cops and their delicate ears and he laughed.

"But one thing I don't understand," David said, "is how did that cop get here so fast? Where in the hell did he come from?"

"He was staked out," Ty said. "You must expect that. I should have warned you. Not that it would have made any difference, probably. It's a common practice in a case like his. You can count on being under pretty heavy surveillance at least until after the trial.

I couldn't bear to think of the trial. "Spies," I said.

"No, Karen. They're here to protect you, too. Nuts come out of the woodwork in cases like this."

We were quiet for a long time.

"I guess I'd better warn the guys in the camp," I said.

"You never saw those people before?"

"Never," David said.

"I only saw her," I said.

"The cop sent the girl to the house afterwards? Alone?"

"Yes. He did. I'd forgotten about that."

"We'd better go through that place with a fine-tooth comb. Can you think of anyone who would want to harm you? Make trouble for you?"

"Have you given up on the land condemnation conspiracy?"

Ty laughed. "The plot thinins. This doesn't smell like the state. They're not above planting a little grass, but the rape bit is a little too far out even for them."

"I've been racking my brain," I said. "We're not the most popular people on the island, but I can't think of anyone who would be so vicious."

"Vicious it is," Ty said. "Yes, ma'm, it's all of that. But don't worry we'll get to the bottom of it."

"I'm not worried," I said.

90

"I am," Ty said. " Do you mind if I spend the night? I'd like to spend another night here. Just to get a feel for the place. We can talk some more, but not now. Tomorrow. We'll eat the big dinner and go to bed. I feel like I've been up forever."

"No macadamia-nut-banana bread," David said.

"No macadamia-nut-banana-bread, " I agreed.

"Why not?" Ty asked. "It sounds delicious."

"Family joke," David said. "Hope to hell she never serves you any."

For the first time that day, Ty looked perplexed.

Lew's Story

By the time David and I got up the following morning, Ty had already left the house. I felt a terrible hostess so got busy in the kitchen making good things for breakfast. Ty's shoes were paired neatly inside the kitchen door, where he'd left them last night, so we knew he hadn't got far.

"Probably went for an early morning jog along the beach," David said.

It was a lovely morning, blue, and gold, and cool.

When Ty came back to the house he was grinning ear-to-ear.

"Cute kids," he said. "But man, I'd hate to have to keep up with them."

"Which kids?"

"Those skiers are sweethearts."

"All those kids are sweethearts, Ty," I shot David a look.

"I'm going to arrange to get them out of here. They only had two weeks."

"And then what?" David asked.

"Well," Ty began and was interrupted by a knock at the door.

"Who is it?" I called.

"It's me, Miz Holt. Lew."

"Can it wait, Lew?"

"Nope. Can't wait. I need ta'talk to you guys. An' Ty Blue." I looked at David and Ty. They nodded.

"Come on in. The door's open." He opened the door and marched in. "How about a cup of coffee? I'll warm some rolls. Homemade jam sound good?"

"Don't go to no trouble on my 'count Miz Holt."

"No trouble. Sit down. Have you met Ty?"

Lew shook his head and shyly extended a thin parchment hand. His fingers were brown and slender. "Pleased to meet'ya," he said.

While I prepared the rolls and jam and got out another cup for coffee, Ty, David, and Lew sat stonily and uncomfortably quiet at the kitchen counter.

Finally Ty cleared his throat.

"Well," Lew began, when I sat down, "I guess I might's as well start in. You kids in a heap a'trouble."

We all nodded.

"Nope. Bigger'n you think. I don't know why but I know what an' that's bad enough. I watched the whole damn shebang."

"What whole damn shebang?"

"Them. That's what. Them creeps. Them guys what done this," he waved his hands around.

'If you saw something why didn't you tell the police?"

Lew snorted and took a bite of roll. He began to talk again with his mouth full. "I don't talk to cops. Prob'ly do you guys more harm'n good anyway."

"You've got a record?"

"Long as your arm," he paused, took another bite, "sure good Miz Holt. Anyways I ain't proud of it but I got it. I was jes-a damn fool kid. Deserved everythin' I got."

"I doubt that," Ty said.

"Heard'bout you, Ty Blue, all the way to West Texas. If it was anyone else sittin' there I wouldn't be sittin' here no matter how much I like Miz Holt."

Ty grinned.

"Jes a smart ass kid. Nobody was gonna tell me how the cow chewed the cabbage, but they did. It was terrible hard on me. Watchin' all them days roll by. Never get'em back, no siree. When they's gone, they's gone. Me. The fresh air kid. Not much fresh air where I was goin'. Swore when I got out I'd never sleep under no roof again."

"Lew! Where do you sleep?"

"Sleepin' bag's good enough fer me. When it rains I move in the barn. Always liked horses. Ain't always been around so many. Wasn't no cowboy, Miz Holt. Shouldn't'a lied. Ust'a dream I was."

"You're the best cowboy I ever knew Lew."

"Go on with your story, Lew. What did you see?" It was easy to see Ty was getting excited.

"I seen'em around the day before the bust. Ugly bunch. Stand-offish. Mean as shit, 'scuse me ma'm, didn't like the looks of'em right off the bat." He took another bite of roll and washed it down with a swig of coffee. "The night of the bust I skedaddled. Takes more'n a army'a'cops to catch ol'Lew in the dark I can tell'ya."

"Why that's right, I said. "I don't remember seeing you at the station."

"That's the last place yur gonna see me if I can he'p it. Anyways, I hid out, figured somebody otta be around to take care'a the animals anyhoo. An'I'seen'em. Busted up the place good. Had fun doin' it. If it hadn't been rainin' they'd burned the place down. Tried...

Watched'em bugger up the house. Hid some grass the cops didn't find. Saw that the night'a'the'party. Should'a told'ya. God, I should'a."

"Never mind, Lew, we wouldn't have known what to make of it anyway."

Lew got up from the counter, went to the fireplace and out from inside the flue drew two sealed bags of marijuana. He handed them to David.

David weighed them in his hand. "Eight ounces at least." David said.

"Dumb place to hide it," I said.

"Never said they was smart," Lew said. "When they set out fer the shop I hightailed it back to the barn. Figured that'd be next."

"Oh, Lew, it was you who saved the horses." I shuddered thinking about what have been.

"Me'an the horses an'chickens an'dogs. Man was them critters in a stew."

"The dogs were scared?" Our three dogs, together, weigh over three hundred pounds.

"Smartest thing they could be. That tall drink'a'water was slashin' a knife around like I ain't seen since stir."

"Where were the police?"

Lew snorted. "If they was around they was sleepin' it off somewhere. Anyways it was really comin' down. Nope. Far as I know there wasn't nobody here but me an'them. Leas'ways I never saw nobody."

"How did you keep them out of the barn?"

"Jes'a little trick I learned in stir, ma'm. I seen a few prison riots, well I seen one prison riot an'that's plenty. Shit, pardon me, ma'm, shit like them guys is usually cowards. Scared'a'their'own'shit. They work in the dark when all the odds're with'em. It must'a sounded like stampede in there. Locked in stall I got'em bellerin'. Locked myself in, too. Made a few funny noises my-own-self," he made a noise like a two hundred pound fighting chicken crowing his last, "'an that did it. We didn't see nobody fer the rest'a'the night an' we was all lookin' and listenin' you better believe. I fed them horses Miz Holt. Prob'ly should'a told ya, but…"

"Oh, Lew, you did wonders as it was. How can I possibly thank you?"

"There's more."

All of us groaned.

"They're still in these parts. Saw'em jes'this mornin'. In town."

"That's the best news I've heard all day," Ty said.

Lew looked doubtful. I looked scared. David looked mad enough to form a necktie party right then and there.

"I don't think we have to worry about them. I doubt they'll ever bother us again. They've done their job. And a good job, too. Now they'll want to get paid. That tall one with the knife interests me. I want you to get that photographer again. He does good work. Hire him. Pay him anything but I want pictures of that bunch. The three of them together, if you can. Lew, will you help?"

"Damn tootin'."

"Okay. If my hunch is correct they'll be splitting. There's only one way off this rock."

"How about by boat?"

"No need worry'bout that Mr. Holt. That's why yur boat weren't harmed. They's sceered a'water. Won't catch those guys surfin' at the beach."

"All of them?"

"Well that tall freaky geek leastaways. He acted like the leader of the pack. All three of'em was pale as the underside of a slug."

"Okay. Hang out at the airport and don't even let one passenger on board without getting a good look at him. Can you do that?"

"Yep."

"One thing. Do you think there's any chance they saw you?"

"Nobody sees ol'Lew when he don't wanna be seen."

"You're sure?"

"I'm here ain't I?"

"Okay. Let's get moving. Things may be opening up for us." Lew nearly knocked his stool over getting up and out the door. "Where are you going? We can call from here."

"You go ahead an' call." Lew called back over his shoulder. "I'm hightailin' it next door. Gotta get to crackin'. Don't wanna lose them leetle buggers now." He clumped down the kitchen steps.

"And so you see, kiddies," Ty said with a grin, "straight shooters always win and the bad guys always get it in the end."

It was old but I laughed anyway.

"An'now before I hightail it back to big citysville ma'm, can I have another cuppa an'a roll? That jam's damn, 'scuse me ma'm, good, ma'm. You know," he took a swallow of coffee, "everyone in that generation was criminal of one sort or another. Only some of us were lucky. Which remind me, how about a share?" He picked up one of the two packages. "Six, eight ounces," he weighed in his hand. "Worth about twelve to sixteen hundred on the street. I'll take it off your bill," Ty said.

He was really examining the package now. "You know this is some of the finest stuff I've seen in a long time. Strange they'd use good stuff. There's a lot of money involved in this somewhere. The cops aren't proud. They'll arrest for leaf as fast as for bud."

"Take it, it's a gift, Ty. Anyway we know you're not going to sell it on a street corner."

Ty picked up one of the packages, stashed it in his attaché case, locked it, and threw me the key. "Mail it to me when you get a chance."

After he left, David and I spent the rest of day lolling around the beach. I evened out my all-over tan and hoped a cop was watching. You'd be surprised what a beautiful little thing I am. If one was there I made sure there would plenty to see. I was still steaming about that middle-age crap.

It was a glorious day to be alive.

The Family

The next day was a stunner.

I got up at five, fed the horses, came back to the house, crawled into bed, seduced David. I love to make him late for work. Got up again at six-thirty, David was still recovering, rode, practiced my yoga, and contemplated my navel for twenty splendid minutes.

I didn't even feel the need to consult the I Ching. Which just proves.

David hauled home an absolutely enormous creation of bleached white driftwood at lunchtime and I made fresh strawberry ice cream with real cream and honey.

It was the first normal day we'd had in weeks.

"Thank God it's Friday," David said when he left for work, minus his pants. "The traffic been a bitch all week."

I was ready for Adams when he called. Everything was opening up on that front, too. He said he'd call back in a day or two and arrange to fly over to talk to us.

"Can't we talk on the phone?"

"No, Mrs. Holt. We can't."

"That bad?"

"Worse. Much worse than you can possibly imagine." He sounded grim.

"Okay. Just let us know. And thanks."

He hung up.

*

David runs a union office. I run a union barn. He takes Saturday and Sunday off. So do my horses. The Queen gave all the horses in England Sunday off, I did her one better.

Sunday we sailed up the North Shore. The sea was flat as a duck pond, but a brisk gentle breeze carried us along. It was more like flying than sailing.

"If it were like this all the time," David said, "we'd be wall-to-wall boats all the way to Waikiki."

"There's always something to be thankful for," I said.

Farther out to sea we watched a school of dolphin jump and spring and frolic. They did not come near the boat. We anchored in our favorite cove, put up a pretty blue awning, and basked like lizards in the sun. I read and drank apple juice. David went for a swim. Later we both swam ashore and walked along the golden beach collecting treasure. Like Caligula, we did Neptune in. There was no one else but us in the entire universe.

Halfway through the day a helicopter full of nosey tourists chased us back into the water. We swam back to the boat and climbed aboard. The people in the helicopter took their allotted run up and down the beach and then climbed back aboard their noisy steed and took off. They circled the boat three times before they flew away. David and I, brazen in our nakedness, ignored them. David was polite he didn't moon them.

"We'll probably hear about this," I said.

"Those goddamned things should be outlawed."

"Then how would people like that ever get a chance to see this beautiful spot?"

"They wouldn't."

"If they knew who we were they'd be thrilled. It isn't every day you get to see the Manson family at play." I got up and strolled to the bow, "You can bet nobody has a camera up there."

"Stop showing off, Karen. They're six of them, there's only one of me."

When they flew away we cheered. David flipped them the bird and we had the cove to ourselves for the rest of the afternoon.

We sailed home late that night, picked up the mooring in the moonlight, made love on the deck. We returned to the house early next morning.

*

Sunday I played around in the barn. Checked Alex's feet. Not bad. Not good. At least he was no longer so ouchy. I cleaned tack. David skimmed along close to shore on the Sailfish. It looked like a lot of fun, but it's an art I haven't mastered. Besides, I'm vain. I don't like muscle. On me.

Kids were loafing on the beach and smells of a feast in the making wafted up from the camp. About noon, Ralph, the blacksmith, showed up unannounced. David had to fix his own lunch.

Together, me doing all the watching, Ralph, dripping sweat, doing all the work, we shod and trimmed twenty hooves. I'd be on Alex's back tomorrow and the thought made me happy. As he packed his gear, lugging the heavy anvil like a leg of spring lamb under one powerful arm, Ralph turned to me and said, "All of us want you to know we believe none of that crap we read in the papers."

"Oh, Ralph, how nice of you to say so."

"And if you need any help you just holler," he bellered as he drove away.

Father called about two. Would we bring flowers with us when we came?

"Sure. You're still determined to go ahead with this?"

"Yes, kitten. I'm telling you that little lady is so sweet she's going to make you cry. Reminds me so much of your mother."

"Do you have in mind any particular kinds of flowers?"

If Adams' story was as good as he seemed to think it was, we'd bring a bunch all right, but I don't know how pretty they'd be.

After dinnertime, Pat, her husband, Ronnie, and our brown-eyed Nalani, appeared.

We all went down to the camp for dinner. Pat and I made buckets of lasagna and garlic bread and carried it between us in a wicker hamper. David and Ronnie carried the wine and beer. Nalani carried the grass. If a cop stopped us anywhere along the way, he'd probably not search a little girl.

"Mom?" Pat said as we walked along.

"Yes, my darling daughter?"

"We want you to know that all that stuff in the papers in just one big pile of bullshit. Everybody knows that."

"I hope so."

"If you need any help, Ma," Ronnie said, "you let me know. I got plenty brothers would like for help."

As we were passing the barn the phone rang.

"Don't answer it," David said.

"It's okay. You go along. It's probably Father again."

Ronnie picked up my side of the hamper and they continued on their way. I went back and answered the phone. It was Tommy, our only son, calling collect. "Mom!" he said.

"Tommy where are you?"

"In the pen."

I groaned. "What now?"

"Those goddam pigs won't let us sell our papers. They've been tearing down our posters, too, and those things cost money."

"Dreadful, Tom. We've been having our share of problems, too."

"Yeah," Tommy said. "Look, Mom, I need…"

"Bail?"

"Hell, no. I'm doing fine."

"I thought you said you were in jail?"

"I am."

"Who's going your bail? Certainly not the Party."

"Mom nobody's going my bail. You don't understand. I'm glad I'm here and I'm staying here."

"In jail?"

"Of course. I'm doing great work here. Organizing the prisoners. These poor men are victims of a vicious and corrupt society. It's a piece of cake, Mom, a piece of cake. But I need money."

"For what, Tom? Don't you like the food?"

"Materials," he said.

"What kind of materials? And how much? I'm not buying guns or knives or hacksaws or even spitballs for the inmates of the Oahu State Penitentiary."

"Oh, Mom, you don't understand, all I need is about twenty-five bucks. I've got to get some cards."

"Cards?"

"Well, hell, Mom, you can't organize without cards. How'll we recognize each other?"

"You could carry a rose in your teeth. Do you want roses? Your grandfather wants roses. I'll send roses."

"Mom, please be serious."

"Okay, I'll be serious. Still you can get an awful lot of cards for twenty-five bucks."

"Well, there's an awful lot of prisoners."

"All right. If it's just for cards I'll write it off to charity. Where do I send it?"

He told me.

"You sure you don't want out?"

"No."

"If you change your mind."

"I don't know what's going on over there but…"

"Try reading the newspapers."

"That reactionary bullshit."

One thing you can say about me, my ears weren't delicate.

"Anyway if you need any help I can send some party members over there. Probably all you need is some good organizers."

"Jesus, Tom, don't send anyone, please!"

I could see those headlines.

CARD CARRYING COMMUNISTS

TO ORGANIZE HIPPY CAMP

"Relax, Mom. I know what a socio-economic backwoods that place is. We won't get around to organizing over there for months. But don't forget I made the offer."

"Oh, I won't Tom. I won't. But please Tommy be careful. There are an awful lot of peculiar people in jail these days. Not all of them, you know, don't deserve to be there."

"I'll be careful. Mom?"

"Yes?"

"You're great and I love you. We all love you. One day you'll be another Rosa Luxemburg."

Marvelous, maybe they'll erect a statue of me in Washington, right alongside Father's.

When I saw David again at the camp, he said, "Who was it this time?"

"Tommy," I said. "He's in jail."

"They ought to consider building one exclusively for the Holt family," David said.

The first day of the week bloomed in all its glory. I rode Alex through a blizzard of Hawaiian dandelion spores, sneezing all the way, and it was heaven.

Lew and the photographer showed up. They got the picture. Good ones, too. Full face. Full length. A pretty mean looking bunch. And they were stupid, or else they thought we were, the three of them left the island together.

I called Ty and he said to send Lew directly to Honolulu. He said to get the pictures to him pronto and he'd take care of everything from there.

Alice called. She wanted to quit school.

"You know what the judge said," I reminded her. "If you were the master mind behind the heist, I think, young lady, you should put that mind to better use." And so Alice enrolled in the School of Architecture designing banks instead of robbing them.

"Yeah but Mom I'm bored to tears."

She was getting straight A's. Winning prizes in photography and art classes and bored to death.

"Read any good newspapers lately?"

"Newspapers?"

"Doesn't anyone read the newspaper anymore?"

"Why should we? You never did."

"Go get yourself some of last week's papers. That should get you out of your doldrums."

"I'll bet."

"Twenty bucks."

"You're on."

"Where'll you get twenty bucks?"

"Rob a candy store, Mom. I'm working my way down in the world. Hey, Mom, I love you."

"I love you, too, Alice." We hung up.

And so we made it through Monday.

Adams

Adams called early Tuesday morning.

"It's a policy of my office, Mrs. Holt, that I only travel first class."

"You've got something that will make all this worth while? We're spending a lot of money, Mr. Adams."

"Guarantee."

"Okay. I'll call our agent as soon as I hang up. Do you want me to have them call you at your office to confirm?"

"That would be acceptable."

"We'll make reservations for you at the Surf. Hopefully we'll have you out tonight. You don't mind flying at night?"

"A night flight is fine."

"We'll pick you up at the airport."

"That won't be necessary, Ms. Holt, but thank you for the offer. I can get to the hotel. I'll call you from there."

"Tomorrow then. And this better be good."

"Three days, Mrs. Holt."

"Three days, Mr. Adams. What have you got, a book?"

He laughed. "You'll be amazed."

"Okay, " I shook my head. David would have to do some high-class inventing.

Adams hung up.

I made the call and got the tickets and reservations. No problem. It was a slow month in the tourist trade. When I finished that chore I wandered down to the barn. Halfway there I encountered our Olympic Team walking up from the camp towards the house.

"We came to say good-bye," their spokes girl said. "Mr. Blue arranged for us to leave and we feel we ought to…" "…but we're not deserting you and Mr. Holt." "We're on your side." "We'll stop by the police station and give our deposition before we go and if you need us we'll be back." "We're also going to see Mr. Blue in Honolulu. He promised to take all of us out to lunch." "We know it wasn't anything you or Mr. Holt did. And we really loved staying here. You're such nice people. We love the way you live." "And, boy, did we have an adventure."

When they all spoke together it was overwhelming. "I haven't got around to calling your parents. Or your coach." I said. "It's awful nice of you to offer but my Dad's an attorney. He knows Mr. Blue. He knows he'd never take a shady case. The fact he's representing you makes you okay in his book and he'll spread the word."

It was a touching farewell scene. Tears and sniffles all around, hearty pats on the back from the girls, a few pats on the fanny from David. David wrote them a fat check and we promised to try to get to the trials. "The skiing trials," David said and the girls laughed.

When they left David threw his arm around me. "They are sweethearts," he said. "Come back," he yelled after them. "Bring your folks. Your coaches. The whole goddam team. Everybody." They turned and waved and disappeared into the forest.

"I can't think of a better bunch to go to jail with," I said.

"With a little bit of luck we won't be doing that anymore," he answered.

I told him about Adam's call and impending arrival. I avoided talking about money.

"This better be good," David said.

"That's what I said, David."

He went back to work and I took off my clothes and went for a swim.

*

Wednesday morning was so beautiful it could have been framed and hung in a gallery. A fresh sea breeze was blowing offshore and there was just enough cloud cover to make the morning nippy. The entire eastern sky was an electric pink trimmed at the top with deep dove gray. The clouds didn't burn off until after ten o'clock and by that time Alex and I were home, cleaned up, and ready to relax. Old Alex bounded out of the barn like a frisky colt and soon all the horses were cavorting around like dolphin in a deep blue sea.

My yoga, which I practiced nude on a raised wooden deck that David built for me in the forest, was one of those rare transcendent moments I frequently, but not frequently enough, experience.

I didn't lift. I floated off the ground. I could have remained standing on my head all morning. It's a terrible confession to make, but often I feel more at home standing on my head than I do standing on my feet. The peacock, an asana that I had practiced diligently for years, was perfect; I was the peacock. I stretched out, my body horizontal to the deck, but six inches above it like a beam, balanced on my forearms, and when I unfolded my gorgeous tail-feathers even the cardinals in the trees took note. Oh, let that damn cop be out there somewhere.

When I meditated my Sahasrara chakra was so charged I could feel the lotus open. My Kundalini Shakti was so powerful I could have run electric trains or bent spoons with my mind. It was after sessions like this that I usually consult the I Ching, but this day I had no questions to ask. I enjoy communicating with the oracle, but I hate to bother her for nothing.

A little more of that, I thought, walking homeward through the forest, and I'd not only stop the aging process, I'd put it in reverse.

David came home for lunch and afterwards both of us went for a swim. The water was the temperature of tepid tea; I could have floated around in it all day. The breeze had stopped, the clouds had dissipated, and the sky was a Van Gogh blue. It would be a hot afternoon.

I went home for a siesta, alone, David went back to work. He had a lot to do to keep financially afloat. When he left he gave me a friendly pat on the fanny, "If Adams calls and we have to go in, let me know. We'll make a night of it. Drinks and dinner. Maybe some dancing. Might as well."

I nodded, and washed and dried my hair before taking a siesta.

Adams called around five. Yes, he had a good flight. Smooth. First class on a 747 was the only way to fly. The flight to Kauai was pleasant. Yes, his room was fine. He laughed. Would we meet him at seven? In his room. He gave me the number.

I called David, fed the animals, and began to dress. We'd have a night on the town. A celebration. God knows we needed one.

*

We had a difficult time finding Adams' room. It was in a wing of the hotel with which we were not familiar. We finally gave up and asked at the desk. After a few minutes, during which several calls were made, the desk clerk gave us directions. "Take the Feathered Cape elevator to the top," he said. "When you get out turn right. You'll see a door marked 'Private'. And a button. Press it."

It all sounded very mysterious to us but we did as we were told. The Feathered Cape is an elegant restaurant on the top floor of the hotel. We'd eaten there often. Before turning right and pushing the button, which, in all the times we'd been up there we'd never noticed, David made reservations for the two of us for dinner.

When we pushed the button a few minutes later, the door opened with a snap. We were surprised, when we passed through, to find ourselves in a long, bright, airy passageway. All the rooms were on the left. On the right was a bank of tall windows looking back towards the mountains. We found Adam's room at the end of the hall.

David knocked.

The door opened immediately. Two local kids in hotel uniforms wearing big, obsequious grins, pardoned themselves and sidled out as we sidled in. I was beginning to feel intimidated, and that was silly, we'd hired this man.

It was an impressive room we entered. The entire wall directly in front of us, a good thirty feet away, was solid glass from floor to ceiling. The shot silk draperies were pulled back and the view across the bay was magnificent. We stood in a small ornate foyer with a wall of gold-veined mirrors on our right, and a long wall, papered in a red-flocked pattern, with one door, closed, to our left.

There was no one but us in the room.

The living room was decorated to the teeth in a phony Hawaiian Regency style. All the furniture was gold brocade and Thai silk. The cocktail table was at least eight-feet long and lacquered a rich deep black.

To the right of the living room was a formal dining room replete with well-stocked bar and burdened with tray after silver tray of food on a gilded buffet. Considering the number of trays, my guess was, we'd missed a few waiters. On the ocean side of the dining room was a bougainvillea-strewn balcony. Off to the other side was a kitchen.

No one was cooking.

It was a transplanted bunny hatch, about as Hawaiian as a Viennese whorehouse.

When the door opened in the red-flocked wall, and Adams walked in, I'm sure our jaws were hanging down.

The sight of the man himself didn't help. He looked like a mammoth leprechaun in a Rudolph Valentino wig. His face was jolly and red and his eyes twinkled. If he hadn't been so damn big I think I'd have laughed. Stick a pipe in his mouth, put a green hat on his head and leggings on his telephone pole underpinnings, then increase the size of everything around him tenfold and be prepared to trick him out of his pot of gold. The black Rudolph Valentino slicked-down wig, slightly askew as though he'd put it on in a hurry, only added to the fun. It made him look like a leprechaun trying to disguise himself as an Arab sheik and failing. He was not entirely sober and his breath fogged the air, I'd get drunk breathing in the air the man breathed out.

"The Holts, I presume," he made expansive gesture and bowed a wobbly bow. "Won't you come in? Be seated, please. Ah, what a delight it is to visit your lovely island. Lovely weather. Lovely room. Lovely company. You are much lovelier than your pictures, Mrs. Holt." He tried another bow. He almost lost his balance and fell. "Come on, you two, sit down. Allow me to buy you a drink. You can't sit around all night with your mouths hanging open. Don't let the place throw you." He laughed.

"No more for you now, Hon. We'll never get to dinner." A voice called from the bedroom. It was the voice on the phone.

"Just keep it down to a college roar, baby. You'll get plenty to eat." He laughed again.

David and I stood rooted to the floor.

"Mr. Adams," I said, "will you please explain what's going on? Who's paying for all this?" I gestured helplessly around.

"Now we don't want to start right out talking about money, honey. How crude. No class. How crass. How inhospitable. A little drinkie-up first." He waggled his little finger on which an obviously phony, very vulgar, man's diamond ring glittered. "You like bourbon, Holt? Or Scotch? Name it we got it," he waved drunkenly at the bar. "You look like a Scotch man to me."

David was speechless. "Cat got your tongue?" Adams said waggishly. "I said sit down."

"Let's get out of here, Karen," David said to me. "If you think we're paying for this, Adams, take another think," he looked Adams squarely in the eye. "You'll be out on your ass before you get that drink poured." He started out the door with me right behind him.

"Don't be so cocky, young man," Adams said. "If I were you I'd hear me out before I did anything rash or thoughtless. You might live to regret it. I'm here to do a little business. Your nickel."

A rumpled-looking blonde in a see-through negligee right out of Frederick's of Hollywood appeared at the open bedroom door. She held a small snub-nosed revolver in her hand. "Just do what the man says, kiddoes. When he says sit, you sit," she said sweetly.

"Ace, honey, why is it always our fate to deal with obstreperous people?"

Adams roared. "You're obstreperous people, did you hear that? Ob-strep-er-ous. Honey bun you're really a charge. Last week you'd have said 'shitty'."

"Shut these people up, do your business, get them out of here, and let's get on with the show." Using the gun as a pointer she pointed to the chairs.

We moved.

We sat.

"Now that's better," Adams said and went on with his drink pouring. You want one?" He said to the blonde.

"When this is over," she said.

Adams set a tall drink in front of David and another just like it in front of me. It might as well have been strychnine. Then he poured himself a drink, walked back into the living room, and seated himself on the sofa.

"This is my first trip to the islands. It was sweety's first ride in an aeroplane, wasn't it kid? Had to hold her hand the whole way. You're lucky people, Holts. Country's going to hell and everybody in it. No peace anywhere. But, ah, the languor of the tropics. I can understand people like yourselves. Dropouts. The ones who run away. Ah, indeed I can. I am not totally without compassion."

"Get on with it, Ace, we'll be here all night. Say what you have to say. He's such an old windbag," she winked at us.

"Yes. Yes. Yes. Business before pleasure. Hand me my brief case, love, it's right behind me on the floor. Drink up," he said to us and drained his glass.

"My. My. My," he said when he received the leather case. He lay it on the cocktail table and opened it with a key. "The Holt family. Tsk. Tsk. Karen," he handed me copies of the Honolulu paper. "Terrible pictures. You really ought to sue. I can recommend a good attorney. You're much prettier than your pictures. Much younger, obviously. Under the circumstances one can understand."

He got up from the table, poured himself another drink, came back and sat down. "Your daughter, now. Alice. Is that correct? Arrested for robbing a Savings and Loan two years ago. Your son, Tom, a notorious rabble-rousing red. He's in jail in Honolulu at the moment. I have a hard time understanding the younger generation but I have no patience whatsoever with the college pinks. Alice, now, I might enjoy. I hear it was an inspired heist. You two, you run a totally disreputable hippy camp out on the North shore. As a family you are, in fact, an infestation. You keep Blue, Holland and Campbell in business."

David swore.

"Shut up," the blonde said. "There's a lady present. Both Ace and me feel that it's good for folks to have to face themselves honestly once in a while."

"That's our function in life is it not Honey Bun?"

The blonde nodded.

"Your father, Karen, is a thief of the old school. A dead beat with a list of bankruptcies this long." He unfolded an accordion sheaf of legal-looking forms as long as the cocktail table.

"And you had the audacity to call me."

The blonde waved the gun.

"Yes, Karen, you had the nerve to call me and ask me to get the goods on the Woodsburys. On Genevieve Fisher, that paragon of virtue. That nice little woman. You really should be ashamed."

David turned to me and started to say something. Adams shut him up. The blonde, still smiling, was lounging against the door, the entire front of negligee open from top to toe. I was proud of David. He didn't even sneak a peek. The gun was still pointed directly at us. It did not waver.

"Now I'll tell you what I'm going to do with you fine folks. Yes, indeed, I will," he shook his finger at us and finished his second drink. This time instead of going back to the bar he reached over and took David's drink. "If you're not going to drink that it'd be a shame to let it go to waste. Fine stuff. The best."

"Make this your last, sweetie, you're beginning to make me nervous."

Adams nodded. "As a kindness, a generosity, it is within my nature to be generous, and it comes right from the heart, I'm not going to tell the Woodsburys about you. And I'm not going to tell that lovely little Mrs. Fisher. If she wants to buy trouble who am I to stop her? No. No. Never say that Ace Adams doesn't mind his own business. But as for the information you seek," he was all Adams on the phone, "I do believe it needs more attention and investigation. In fact, who knows when it will end? I'll send a bill every week, you have payment on my desk…"

"…my desk," grinned the blonde.

"…before the week is out and I won't say a word about your scandalous Daddy and your infamous selves. And if you get any smart ideas about informing the police about our business arrangement, well I might have to tell them in truth you hired me to blackmail all those nice folks back home. Who in the hell would ever believe your story? Would you like some of these clippings for your scrapbook? I've got copies of everything in my office in case you should get some other funny ideas. When one is dealing with a pack of criminals like you one can never be too careful."

He smiled. They both smiled.

"Okay get!" The blonde said.

"Now! Now! Remember your manners."

The blond pointed us towards the door with her little gun.

We left. We even turned our backs on the gun. It didn't take courage. Only a madman would shoot his meal ticket in the back. We made as gracious an exit as we could, considering the circumstances. We didn't slam the door. Just before the door oozed shut we heard them laughing.

"Cute kids," the blonde said.

"Not as cute as you, kid," Adams answered.

In the hallway we bumped into the two waiters who, with not quite so much consideration this time, wheeled two dinner carts by us.

"Well, David," I said, "I can sure pick'em."

David nodded, but he was kind. "We made a mess of that," he said. We didn't bother to cancel our reservations for dinner.

We didn't stop for a drink.

I would have to look more carefully at that detective bit in the I Ching. I bet David would check the figures he punched into his Kepnor-Tregoe, too.

Lorraine

The drive home took forever, although there were few cars on the going in either direction. Ahead and behind us was nothing but a black and empty stretch of highway.

"I hate the thought of blackmail, David. If the bride and her family are as decent as everyone says surely we can risk telling them the truth. I mean it's all preposterous."

"All except your dad's past, Karen."

"And Tommy and Alice," I sighed. "Some people might not understand."

"It would be a risk. It all depends on how much you think of your dad."

"I love my Father."

"What if she didn't understand? I take it this marriage, this woman, is important to him."

"She's important, David, but is she that important? That man Adams could drain us dry."

"No. It isn't that bad. As soon as they're married we stop payment. Adams can tell her anything he wants then. She'd find out about Charlie sooner or later anyway."

"Could be a short marriage, David." "Could be. Jesus, they're both in their seventies. At best it isn't going to break any longevity record."

" It means giving up the land."

"It's his."

"But, David, we, you, have a fortune in it. Besides half of it is mine. Mother left it to me. That would be giving to my Father's new daughter that which Mother gave to me and that's awful. She'd flip in her grave."

"She isn't in a grave," David said, and that was true. Mother was in the air, we'd had her cremated and scattered her ashes in the valley.

We drove silently down the hill. The mountains ringing our valley were dark sentinels guarding the sparkling silver necklace that was the river. Everything was dark in our sleepy little town except the New Papeete, which was lit up like the fourth of July. We could hear voices inside singing. On the verandah, Lorraine's Japanese lanterns spun and twinkled in the breeze.

Suddenly David swung the car around. "I promised I'd take you out to dinner and out to dinner we shall go. The hell with it! Fuck it! Fuck the whole fucking mess."

We parked in front of Lorraine's bar and restaurant and put on happy faces. We forced ourselves to look carefree and gay as we strolled hand-in-hand up the steps. Great, beautiful, warm-hearted Lorraine came out to greet us. "I got good shrimp. An' choc-lat cake. A bottle of white wine…"

We grinned. Shrimp, white wine and chocolate cake were exactly what the occasion called for. We swore to each other, with our eyes, to speak no more of our misfortunes that night. We joined the noisy band of revelers in the bar and waited for Lorraine to call us for dinner. I had a large mai-tai. David had two. We drank these down and ordered the same thing once again to take with us in to dinner.

It wasn't long before Lorraine came to get us and after she'd checked to see the party in the bar was well on its way, joined us at the table. Our small talk was anything but scintillating in spite of the wine Lorraine kept pouring and mai-tais we kept sipping in between. The curried shrimp, as I recall, was delicious.

Another bottle of wine and half another order later we spilled the beans. Lorraine, great heart, just sat there and listened. It was I who first began to babble, but it was David who told the entire tale, embellished, embossed. He wrapped it in fine parchment and tied it with a big red ribbon.

"So we're all going to jail on trumped charges of possession and rape and getting blackmailed for them, too." He took a bite of shrimp, a bite of chocolate cake, and washed the whole thing down with a glass of wine followed by sips of mai tai. He poured himself another drink.

It struck me as such an interesting combination of tastes, I tried it, too. It was only sort of interesting but I didn't gag.

Lorraine sat there, her shell-like ears defenseless against David's barrage of words. She took it all in for a long time ignoring the ruckus in the bar-over there it was beginning to sound as though the party was getting rough-and then she began to twitch. She wiggled around in her seat like a nursery school kid too shy to ask the teacher. She wrung her hands. Her head nodded and bobbed. She looked like a big old-fashioned wind-up doll that had come unsprung. Lorraine, a lady of rare restraint, was coming unglued.

I took another swallow of wine, "Lorraine if you have to go to the bathroom you may." I motioned towards the lady's john.

The crowd in the other room was beginning to sound demented. The other diners, who'd been with us in Lorraine's native art gallery of a dining room, had already drifted off in the direction of the bar We heard a crash, a sour note on a guitar, a voice raised in anger.

"Go now" Lorraine said and stood up.

We nodded. Both of us had interpreted this to mean she was going. It sounded as though she were needed in the other room. She is not facile with the English, her accent is a bit heavy, and the liquor we had in us didn't make it any easier to translate. We kept on eating. And drinking. David tried the shrimp, cake, and wine combination again. He polished off the wine in his glass and reached for the bottle Lorraine had brought us.

"No! You eat you drink. Enough. Go home," she said 'g'ome'. "It's too late for Lorraine. You no t'ink I needs sleep, too? Li'sen to dem in dere. Bye'n'bye cops come. Bod crowd." She began to clear the table. Plates, half full, disappeared. The bottle of wine she'd given us was whisked away. The tablecloth went next in a grand breadcrumb, cake-crumb flourish. I sneezed.

It was an unusual performance. Lorraine's hospitality is as generous as her bulk. We'd never heard her ask anyone to leave. She can calm a rowdy crowd with her eyes. Tonight, however, she meant what she said. David, hurt, pulled his wallet out of pants. "No," she shook her head. "Pay tomorrow. You come again some other time."

I shook my wine-and-rum-befuddled head. She certainly did want rid of us in the worst way. Well, poor dear, we'd probably taxed even her educated heart. How much garbage can one soul listen to without getting fed up?

"I'm really very," I hiccupped, "sorry. Lorraine." I wanted to cry I felt so bad. To top off the day we'd alienated our best friend. She was sweeping us before her and pushing us firmly out the door.

We tumbled down the stairs, staggered to the car, and climbed in. As we drove off we could see, behind us, other bodies being propelled into the night. She'd had enough of everybody, I guess.

"It just gets worse, David."

"I'll make it up to her tomorrow."

"I hope tomorrow never comes," I blubbered. David looked sad.

"It's never so bad it can't get worse," he said.

*

We didn't stop at the camp, although a party was in full swing there, too. We could see people in silhouette gathered around a bonfire. Naked girls were dancing in a circle. When we got to the house, we didn't light the lamps. When we got in bed, we didn't make love.

Both of us lay on our own side of the road waterbed as alone and remote from each other as castaways on two deserted islands. I didn't fall asleep until the sky started turning gray, and the birds, those nasty creatures, began to screech. I was no sooner asleep than I was shaken awake again. Someone was banging at the door downstairs.

"I'm going to kill myself," I groaned.

David groaned back.

"It's daylight. It can't be the cops," I said and put a pillow over my head. Lorraine's wine and all those mai-ties were dreadful things to my Sahasrara, to say nothing of my head. The door banged again.

"Kar'en time you gets up."

I perked an ear. The voice called again. "Kar'en!"

"That sounds like Lorraine," I said. "What would she be doing here this time of day?"

"She wants money."

"Don't be mean, David, just because your head hurts. She's probably sorry about the whole thing and brought us some chocolate cake so we can make up and be friends."

"I'll settle for wine," David said. "Late brunch."

"Lorraine?" I called down.

"Come down. Op'n door. I make coffee. You dress."

When she walked in the foundation trembled. She looked as awful as I felt. She was wearing the same clothes she'd worn the night before, a table-cloth-like sarong. It looked as though she'd slept in it. "I'm sorry, I said, "I have a horrible headache."

"I feex. You dress. Wiki wiki."

"I'm comfortable in my robe, Lorraine," I yawned and tried to stretch. It hurt like hell. "Make the coffee. Quietly. I'll watch."

"No. Put pants. We go."

"Go? Where go? I just got up."

"Never mind. Go." She was very agitated. Perhaps she felt bad about last night. I decided it was easier to humor her than to fuss. I'd put on a pair of jeans, a shirt, and we'd talk it over. "The coffee and the pot are on the counter. Help yourself. Don't bang them." I clambered up the stairs.

"What's going on?" David wanted to know.

"Who knows? She doesn't want you to put pants on. She wants me to put pants on. If she wanted you to put pants on she'd be up here putting your pants on. Or screaming at you. She's not, so obviously she doesn't want you to. That should be clear."

"Clear," David said careful not to shake his head. "I can't understand a damn thing you're saying."

I made a sound like a half-drowned rain-drenched cat.

"What's she want? What's she doing down there. My God it isn't even seven o'clock."

" I don't know what she wants. She's making coffee. She's banging pots. And I'm not responsible for the position of the hands on the clock."

"What kind of an answer is that?"

"Oh, David, how do I know? I don't know what she wants. I can hardly understand a word she says. She says, 'you dress', 'you go'. I dress I go I'm not strong enough to argue. And those goddam birds."

I hitched up my pants, slipped on a pair of zoris, and ran my fingers through my hair. I just let it hang. What the hell. Days that start out like this only get worse. I might as well look the part.

"I'm off to where I'm off to." I said. "If I don't return someday don't call the cops. Maybe Adams going to kidnap me and demand a ransom."

"Brush your teeth. Wash your face." David said.

"Screw you. If one more person orders me to do one more thing in my own house this morning, one, or possibly two more persons are going to be kicked out of here on their collective fat asses." I said it loud enough for Lorraine to hear. I clumped down the stone stairs as best I could clump in my rubber slippers, and walked into the kitchen.

"Stop clumping," David said, "and don't expect to be ransomed any time soon."

Lorraine was all sweetness and light. She beamed at me showing all those beautiful white teeth. They were so white they made my head hurt.

"You look pretty," she nodded. "Good coffee. You like fo'drink one cup before we go?"

I forgot to be angry and smiled. "Okay. One cup and we go. Am I allowed to know where?"

She shook her head.

"Why?"

"She shook her head again. "Good coffee, no?" she nodded.

"Good coffee, yes. After it's all over do I get a piece of that good choc-lat cake we didn't get enough of last night?"

She nodded and grinned.

I drank my coffee and went.

No handcuffs.

*

Lorraine decided it was best we take my car. "I no got plenty gas enough," she said. "You gots?"

"I gots," I said.

"Okey. Dokey. We go."

Okay. Dokay. We went.

She navigated. We drove past the Post office, the New Papeete, and headed up the road towards town. It was a beautiful morning, the coffee and all the fresh air, plus Lorraine sitting alongside me like a great Polynesian idol, helped restore my

127

spirits. I could see a sail stark white against the sky, way out on the horizon. I pointed it out to Lorraine.

"You'll have a rowdy crowd tonight. Not all to be local."

She grunted.

At the outskirts of Kapaa we turned up the hill. At Mahelona, our local hatchery, we turned right again. I parked where Lorraine directed, in a long row of empty stalls, in a section marked 'Visitors'. The place looked deserted.

"Here? " I asked.

She nodded.

"Am I committing you or are you committing me?"

She didn't answer.

"Come," she opened the door, got out, and beckoned me to follow.

I followed.

We went up the stairs into the main building. Lorraine waved to a nurse behind the reception desk and kept right on walking. Several corridors and several desks later we turned into an unmarked room. It was a long dreary room with six gray-painted beds lined up under the high window. All the pitiful little beds were neatly made and empty. Except for one.

One lonely figure sat hunched over, his back to us, on the bed farthest from the door. Just sitting there he looked forlorn and hopeless. His pajama bottom didn't match his tops, and the strings holding the top part together were either untied or missing.

I didn't want to take one more step. My life was already filled with enough calamities. Lorraine had to push me forward.

The figure on the bed turned his head and looked up at me with great soulful eyes. I couldn't believe it. "Mrs. Holt," he said and then he looked at Lorraine. "You promise me that she's not one of them. You must swear to me before I say another word."

I turned to Lorraine. She shook her head. "Kar'en not one of'em."

"You swear Mrs. Holt," he whispered.

I didn't know what to say. Lorraine gave me a nasty jab in the side. "I don't know who it is you think I am or might be but I swear I am your friend."

He sighed. "They would never say it that way. I have a confession to make, Mrs. Holt."

Just what I needed, a deathbed confession in a nut house. "Call me Karen."

He nodded. "I wasn't the first, Karen, and I probably won't be the last, but, no, don't say anything, you must trust me, I am really your friend, too, and you need one right now." I nodded. "First of all I deceived you, I am not really a gypsy." I just stared. "Nor a violinist, either." This was ridiculous. "My real name, Karen, is Jasper Johns Fisher."

It took Lorraine and me the better part of the morning to get Jasper, for that's what he asked us to call him, out of there. The Gods that be did not consider him dangerous. They were pleased to see him go. For his sake. He'd not give them any trouble. They did not consider him dangerous. Disoriented, but harmless. We spoke to two shrinks, several nurses, and the hospital administrator, and signed a raft of papers. The fate of Jasper Johns Fisher, the late gypsy

Jake, was in our hands.

At last we were given his clothes. I don't know what became of his violin, Alex wouldn't miss it. After Jasper finished dressing, we left the hospital.

He began to tell me his story on the way home. Lorraine had already heard it.

I could hardly believe my ears.

Jasper Johns Fisher

The driver, a black man, though not attired in livery was dressed neatly enough. His black trousers were creased and new looking, no shine in the seat, no frayed cuffs. His white shirt was starched and crisp and a perky bow tie, clip on, stood at attention under his chin.

His patent leather shoes, boots really, were polished to a fare-thee-well. He could see his reflection in the toes.

The limousine, black and long in the body as the man himself, glistened from many rubbings. His boss, lounging in the soft gay suede of the back seat, tried to be attentive. Failed. Tried again.

"These are bad parts for a black man. I can tell you, boss. Folks in these parts come right out of the hills. Bare-assed. They're as goofy and inbred as some of those ding-alings down south."

"You're talking like a bigot, Boots. A black bigot."

"Sometimes there's truth in bigotry, Jasper."

Jasper Johns Fisher grinned. "Sometimes you're right. Stop here for a moment friend and look up there. That's mine. We'll build the house at the top of that hill and I promise when we get up there no one in this sleepy town will bother you."

"Got to come down sometime," the black man snorted. "If for no other reason than just to buy shoe polish."

Boots and his wife held out for three months and then took leave. When they left Boots said, "Mr. Fisher I've liked working for you. You're a good man but I can't take anymore of this. As a friend let me give you a piece of advice, all's not what it looks like down there. I can't put my finger on it but it stinks. You watch your step, you hear? All I smell in this town is trouble and more trouble. Big trouble."

Jasper smiled, although he was sad to see the man go. "I've watched my step all my life, Boots. I'll miss you. And Tildy. I'll be careful I promise. If you ever need a hand, let me know. Hal's a good man so I won't worry about you. Wouldn't worry about you anyway. You're a survivor, friend. If you ever want to come back."

"Here? Forget it man. This berg's Doomsville city."

Jasper didn't feel as cheery as he tried to look. He wasn't superstitious and he didn't believe black men were any more sensitive than white men, nevertheless Boots had insight, always had, and Jasper paid attention to thing like that.

The first day they'd drive through the town, where Fisher had decided to move his headquarters, a feeling had prevailed. He felt it at the service station where they'd stopped for gas. At the restaurant where they'd had lunch. At the bank where he'd opened an account. It was nothing he could put his finger on. The people stared. That was to be expected. But they were hard stares, narrowed behind veiled half--closed eyes. There were no direct look, only shifty glances.

There were no other black people in town, at least none that he'd seen, and Boots, too, had done some looking, so that was part of it. There were no limousines, either; doubtless they posed a threat. Still there was something distinctly hostile and threatening behind those hard looks. Those icy eyes. Those fishy smiles.

Jasper passed it off as pure provincialism. This area was, or it had been, before the new highway slashed its way through, a pretty remote backwater. "They'll get to like us, Boots," he said. "Especially when we start writing all those checks."

The town could obviously stand some sprucing up, and sprucing up took money. In its present condition it was run down and shabby. There was no life or enthusiasm anywhere. There was only decay and distrust.

There was one decent dwelling, an old stone mansion surrounded by acres of manicured gardens, and walls, and heavy, formidable wrought iron gates.

From an upstairs window, as the limousine passed below her on the street in front, Genevieve Raleigh watched. She took off her diamond-flecked glasses and swung them on her long-nailed thumb. Her big golden eyes, still bright and beautiful at sixty-four, narrowed charmingly. "How exciting, Bessie. A new boy in town."

"Now mother," her daughter said.

*

When he left the Vancouver operation, Jasper used every device known to management to get his best friend and plant manager, Hal Barlow, to come along with him to the new locale. He'd get another man for Vancouver, he needed Hal with him.

"It's beautiful country, Hal. You can pick up a lot of acreage cheap. There's nothing you can do here that you can't do there. Plus you'll be close to the kids now they've gone away to school."

"Not on your life," Hal laughed his booming laugh. I was born in this town and I'm going to die in this town. We got rid of the kids. They don't want Mom and Pop camping in their backyard anymore than we want to be there. Let'em test their wings. Nope, I can do more for you right here than I could ever do down there. With you out of here and busy with the new project, and all the trouble that entails, you're going to need someone you can trust. Someone who knows the business inside and out. Someone you won't have to worry about. You'll have enough worries without that. I admit that's a better, more central location, but I ain't goin'. If you need some handholding, just call, I'll fly down. I can be here in a couple of hours, but I'm flying right back."

The man had a smile as big as giant Sequoia and a heart to match. His head was large and his eyes sparkled with wit and intelligence. His shoulders were so wide all his jackets had to be tailor-made; no off- the-racks for Hal.

Behind the desk, below the waist, however, it was another story. His tiny feet barely touched the floor. Even in his built-up shoes he stood scarcely five-feet tall. As long as Jasper had known him, and that was a long time, they'd been friends, boyhood friends in the timber country together. Jasper was still shocked when Hal stood alongside him and he realized how short the man actually was.

Yet he was the biggest man Jasper John Fisher had ever known, with a bigness of spirit which is a much rarer quality than mere height.

Hal rose now and moved around the desk. "Find a me with long legs you skinny bastard. I'm staying right where I am."

Jasper sighed, but accepted defeat. He couldn't afford to lose a man like Barlow. 2

*

It was decidedly peculiar, then, when Jasper met Owen Woodsbury. By God if he wasn't almost that, a long-legged

Barlow. Oh, there was a weakness, the chin was not quite so pronounced, nor the eyes so bright, yet there was a resemblance. The odds of the man being as intelligent were slim, of course, but that would be true of almost any man. He was not witty nor big-hearted, but that, Jasper thought charitably, could be as much a fault of his training as it was a lack of character.

Jasper, for luck then, he'd already lost Boots, stole Owen away from the chamber and made him general manager of Fisher enterprises.

Jasper was the wealthiest lumber baron in the Northwest. It was a feather in Owen's cap. No one could have been more honestly delighted than his mother-in-law, nor more deeply perplexed than Owen.

Owen's bad heart, the reason for his early retirement, was certainly part of his misfortune, but not all of it, and he'd finally ended up back here in Sticksville, U.S.A., living with his formidable mother-in-law, the Genevieve Raleigh, in that white elephant she called a house, taking charity to keep him and his wife comfortable in their coke habit and pornographic movie and book collection.

He had many make-do jobs, thanks to the weight his mother-in-law pulled in this berg, and they paid well, but he and Bess had been accustomed to better things. Things not especially known for their abundance in the backwoods.

Only an idiot could have come out of the job he had in Vietnam with plebian tastes. The only fly in the ointment was Jenny, she terrorized him.

Him! Colonel Owen Stoddard Woodsbury, West point, Class of '49, solid middle, a man who'd found his nitch killing and ordering men to kill, terrified by a tiny little woman.

"Good grief, Owen, can't you breath with your mouth closed? Your adenoids are showing."

"Mother!" Bess would exclaim which only made it worse.

"I'd rather he walked around with his fly open. He looks like the village idiot. Is it a sinus problem or what? I'm ashamed to be seen on the street with him."

"You look like the goon," was another favorite endearment. "Didn't they teach you how to stand up straight in that silly Army? What did they teach you anyway?"

"They taught me to kill, Mother Raleigh."

"Kill what, Owen? Unarmed women and children? You're a ninny and you're beginning to get on my nerves."

Jenny was careful to keep most of her business dealings to herself. She would not have Owen involved in any of her moneymaking ventures. So, she gave him to the town, and then, so she thought, to Fisher.

"He must be a fool," she said once about Jasper's choice of managers. "Looks are often deceiving. And yet there is all that money."

*

Jenny was born in August 1906. Her mother was a wide-eyed German servant girl fresh out of the old country who died in childbirth. Had you asked she could not have selected who, of her many bed partners, had fathered her child.

The baby was beautiful. Perfect in every detail. Her diminutive ears were porcelain petals set in a bloom of golden ringlets which encircled her fine little head like a cap. Her eyes were enormous and of such a light luminous brown they could be called golden. Thick curly black lashes swept adorable rosy high-boned cheeks. She was born with classic features.

Her stepmother cut her lashes off once in a fit of jealous rage, but, to her dismay, they grew right back.

Newborn Jenny had been adopted by the local preacher and his wife. They had christened the child Genevieve Anne. The burly minister perambulated her around as proudly as he stalked the dark alley minds of his flock of local sinners. He got to hear all the juicy gossip that he didn't get to buy in the town's non-existent porn shops.

His wife, a girl from Southern California, hated the child. "Not only do I have to be buried in this whistle stop, I have to play nursemaid to some snot of a servant girl's bastard child." She married the preacher because he was the only man who asked her. She never quite became the proper submissive Christian wife. Except in public.

"That or back to one nightstands in L.A. Lou," her husband replied pleasantly enough and threw the family Bible in her face. He wasn't much of a preacher man, either. Except in public.

Jenny's early years were a vivid contrast in over-indulgence and child abuse. She learned early she could get anything she wanted from her adoring stepfather. She also learned how to instigate arguments and fights between him and his wife. For every blow Emmy Lou gave Jenny, Emmy Lou received two from her husband. She sometimes wore dark glasses to church and almost always wore a long sleeved jacket or top.

When her stepfather died of the flu in 1918, Jenny was a nubile twelve. The entire town and folks from miles around mourned her father; he'd been a charismatic preacher and public figure. The funeral was something the little girl would never forget. It was in the winter and the yellow chrysanthemums, which covered the casket, were bejeweled with frozen drops of dew.

"At least I won't have you, you prize bitch, to bugger up my life anymore," Emmy Lou said after the funeral and took her last black eye, a hefty insurance check-premiums she'd bought with her own hopeful money-and a satchel filled with small denominations from town's people-back to L.A. where she opened a bar, happy to be the widow of a dead but not forgotten preacher man, happy to get the hell out of there.

Jenny, left behind, allegedly until the widow got her feet back on the ground, was the pride of the community. Real beauties were rare. When her stepmother left she moved in with the local banker and his brood. She was sweet, natural, and kind. She still sang in the church choir in a clear little-girl soprano, and she loved to tend the sick. Sickness fascinated Jenny. The dying sent her into fits of rapture. She stuck around for almost half a year, tolerant of the banker's lovely family, and then when a telegram arrived announcing the demise of her dear departed mother, she invented an adoring aunt, a long lost sister of her father's in Seattle, so the banker, his family, and the kindly town's people wouldn't worry or attempt to detain her, and got the hell out of there, too.

It was in the railroad station in Seattle that she met with and joined Dr. Anyll Roberts, a man in his early fifties, a specialist in catarrh, colic, constipation, and hookworms. He also treated hogs, horses, mules, and delivered calves. With him Jenny traveled to Portland.

Dr. Roberts liked his women young, but small towns offered little opportunity to indulge his passion. Jenny, the dear beautiful child, was perfect. He passed her off as the daughter of a deceased sister in Sioux City Falls, and no one was the wiser. A child as angelic, as filled with good deeds as Jenny, was above suspicion.

Old Doc was a snake-oil-salesman par excellence who lived to a virile sixty-five. He'd have lived a decade or two longer had he trusted Jenny less. A doctor's office is a treasure trove of drugs and deadly potents.

He died, leaving to his dear, sweet niece, now a glowing twenty-four, twelve hundred acres of prime farm land, a house around which an entire township would one day develop, and fifty thousand dollars cash in a Portland bank. Not bad for a little girl who'd come out of the sticks twelve years before with sixty dollars in a straw bag and two steamer trunks full of hand-me-down dresses.

Jenny, whose innocent exterior belied her errant ways, was no longer a favorite of the ladies, church choir or not. It was not jealousy, although she was a beauty. It was a secret something, an unexpressed knowledge the ladies of the town could not have identified had they tried, but they knew something evil lurked behind those golden eyes.

All the men, on the other hand, adored her. But them she kept at a wide-eyed distance. She'd had her fill of dirty old men.

In 1934 she met and fell head over heels in love with another doctor, a young doctor this time, Dr. Richard Raleigh, from two towns farther north. Dr. Ritchie, as he was fondly called by the townspeople, was as handsome, broad-shouldered and dark, as Jenny was beautiful, petite, and fair. They were a comely couple, the pride of the community.

Only Ritchie's mother knew what Jenny was and she wasn't telling. She also knew what her son was.

The day after the wedding she moved to Mexico City. "With you two paired up," she said, "I'd get off this damn continent if I could, but I can't. I get seasick." She departed resplendent in her frippery, waving her feathered boas, flashing her gaudy rings.

In 1935, Jen and Doc Ritchie established a home for elderly gentlemen in the newly incorporated township. Nestled in the midst of green rolling lawns, the big white structure was open, cheery, and drafty. Pneumonia stalked the halls.

After an old timer had turned his life savings, his land, and all his possessions over to Ritchie and Jan, he'd slip rapidly away. It's a peaceful death, pneumonia, or at least it was with Jenny, the beautiful angel of death in attendance, administering with soft hands and softer voice to the poor hallucinating dears. Anyone watching her move among the sick and dying would have kissed her feet or polished her halo. The expression on her face was one of exquisite torment tinged with bliss. The Anyll Roberts memorial Home for the Aged had become the place to go. And die.

Once in a while, Ritchie and Jen would get lucky and some rickety old geezer, really loaded to the gills, would come in from the big city to die. There was never any trouble. For years the pair of them fooled, bribed, or blackmailed the best health inspectors the state had to offer.

Old men stood in line to die at the Anyll. They didn't have long to wait.

In 1935, Jan and Ritchie's only child was born. A girl. They named her Bessie Mae. She was not a beautiful infant. She was not a beautiful child. She grew up to look like her father. Big everywhere. Her legs were solid oak. Her arms were kegs of beer. Her hair was dirty-mouse brown and her eyes were a nasty shade of hospital green. They were the exact color, Jenny was quick to note, of something one might find settled to the bottom of a chamber pot in a cholera ward.

Bessie had an aristocratic nose, thin, and well formed, set at an odd angle somewhere above and between a mean and hateful mouth.

Jenny packed this doltish horror off to a school as far and as fast as she could. Jenny could not stand children and Bess would have taxed the patience of the most ideal of ideal mothers.

Bessie, for all the years at the Miss Nelson Academy for Young Ladies, was the most disliked girl in school. Other girls were afraid of her. She liked best to hunt sparrows with slingshots and set kitten's tails on fire to watch them run themselves to death. She also loved to pop pimples, of which she had abundance on her jutting chin. She was cruel and cunning, stupid and sly.

When she left the Academy, the head mistress said, "You won't have us to restrain you any longer, Bessie May. But hopefully you will have others. All we can do is pray."

To her mother she said, "it would be a blessing if she had no children, but if she does don't send them to us. We did the best we could. We failed. We don't care to be reminded."

Jenny understood. She had no desire to become a grandmother anyway so Bessie, under Ritchie's clumsy knife, in the Anyll Robert's tiny surgery, had her appendix removed. She would have no children.

The world at least was safe from that.

Bessie was gleeful.

Owen, who she tumbled in the bushes a full ten minutes after they met, fell madly in love with her. Up until the time he met Bessie, he'd never had the courage to express his own buried sadistic pleasures. West point did that much at least. Bessie undid it. The pair of them had a picnic in Vietnam.

In Nazi Germany, they'd have made beautiful lampshades together.

When Jenny was fifty-four, she caught old Doc Ritchie in a compromising position, to say the least, with a newly hired fresh-faced nurse in an unused examination room.

Jenny complimented her husband on his imaginative use of the facilities and could hardly wait her turn. She was very civilized about the whole affair. Nevertheless poor old Doc found himself very dead of mysterious causes, complicated by a bout of pneumonia, within the year.

The young nurse was taken in by Jenny's sophisticated, but saintly ways, until she, too, developed symptoms. And by that time it was too late. She finished her young life in the county Home for the Insane. "Mad as a hatter," the doctor who committed her proclaimed.

Jenny had discovered mercury. Thermometers, after all, were everywhere.

*

In 1970, when Jasper Fisher had arrived, she'd been widowed for ten years. It was almost too easy for a widow to hoodwink lonely old men and Jenny looked lovely in black.

"But enough is enough," Jenny said.

By that time she'd acquired more land than she could sell and more money than she could spend.

She had social standing. She was the matriarch of the town. She had beauty still, her looks, like fine old wine, had mellowed, not aged. She knew where all the bodies were buried and collected a closet full of the town's dirty linen. She was blackmailing the Mayor, the entire city Council, one of them a woman, the Chief of Police and the County Coroner.

Both the town pubs, one for the geeks, one for the gentry, belonged to her. As did the local Madam and her girls. She owned the town, from the top of the elegant, if slightly tipsy Tower of Pisa church spire, to the depths of an extensive drug underground.

She was President of the town's Historical Society-fantasy fictionalized- and after she married Jasper and moved up the hill, the old Raleigh home became a local museum. There weren't enough closets there to hold all the town skeletons. Owen and Bessie moved out, on Fisher's generous salary they could afford a home of their own.

The Dr. Richard Raleigh Museum was Jenny's pet project. It was a jumble of bones and worthless memorabilia.

The Raleigh's rosewood dining room table, inlaid with ivory and mother-of-pearl, stood in a room all by itself, alongside another room which contained the very same table, stirrups and all, upon which old doc and Nurse Ellen consummated their fateful alliance.

The walls in this room were a mass of photographs of wrinkled old men and the women who attended them. Nothing quiets a dying old man quite like a bevy of pretty young girls. The Judas goats who led these men to slaughter were Bunnies before their time.

Jenny claimed the room had great social and historical significance.

Jenny's wedding dress, under glass, and dripping seed pearls, adorned a manikin made up to look like her as a young woman. "Only not as pretty," the old folks in the town said loyally.

Jenny chaired the Friends of the Symphony, although she disliked classical music, the Friends of the Ballet, although she considered the ballet too cute for words. She thought Owen would look sweet in a tutu and loved to tell him so. She was benefactress of the zoo, although she detested animals. She also supported a home for unwed mothers and a home for juvenile delinquents. There was not much going on in the town that Jenny did not have a dainty finger in.

When Jasper arrived she was ready for a change. She'd conquered all the fields there were to conquer and was feeling bored with it all. "Challenge is the spice of life," she said to Bessie, "and I'm challenged by all that money."

For Jasper it was love at first sight.

*

Lorraine and I settled Jasper into a sleeping nook alongside the fireplace in the living room. This afternoon, even with the plastic windowpanes, the room looked bright. The plants seemed to thrive in the light.

I made a pitcher of magic juice, lots of wheat germ, lots of Brewer's yeast, lots of orange juice, bananas, and honey. When Jasper made a face after the first swallow, I bribed him with two oatmeal-raisin-carob cookies.

"You have to recover your health, Jasper, and you haven't much time. That's our first concern. Take a little nap now." I handed him a whole fistful of vitamins and watched him swallow every one. "When David comes home this evening you're going to have to go through the whole painful business again. I want you to tell him exactly what you told us. Leave nothing out."

"And the rest of the story, too, Karen," he said.

Lorraine, who hadn't left Jasper's side since we got home, took a bite of my cookie, made a face. "I go get some cake," she said. She wasn't high on health food.

When David came home I met him at the door. "Keep your pants on," I said, "we have company." I hugged him anyway, kissed him, and pulled him along by he arm into the living room. "I want you to meet someone, darling," I said.

*

Jasper, lying in the snuggle, looked embarrassed. "I've played the fool so long I hardly know how to act around normal people."

"Don't worry," David said, "nobody around here's normal."

"Does he know who I am?" I shook my head. "I'm Jasper John Fisher," he said extending his hand.

David looked perplexed.

Jasper moved right into the preamble and that began the part of the story neither Lorraine nor I had heard. We sat spellbound. Jasper told the story with much dramatic embellishment, the man was a consummate actor and a much better story teller than a violinist.

"I wish you could have seen her then. She was as beautiful as any little beauty queen. Let's see, that was 1970, she must have been sixty-four. At sixty-four she was prettier than most women half her age.

"That doesn't add up, Jasper," I said counting on my fingers," that would make her seventy. She told me she was seventy-five."

"She lies about her age," Jasper said. "She told me the same thing, but I know for a fact she was born in 1906.

If you could cross Marlene Dietrich with Marilyn Monroe, make it pint size, she's a tiny little thing, age her a bit and pile a mass of curls on top, you'd almost have her. Except for the eyes. They got bigger and more golden the entire time I knew her. She's had her face lifted and her eyes done, too, she told me that, she wasn't shy about it. But it wasn't the lack of wrinkles that impressed you most- it was the color of those eyes. I never saw anyone with golden eyes before. Haven't seen anyone since.

You two young kids – you, too Lorraine – you can't imagine what it's like to fall in love for the first time at sixty-five. I was always so busy making money and carving an empire for myself I never had time for love. I was a pretty rough country kid, right out of the tall timber and I was going places. Nothing was going to stop me, slow me down, hold me back. You go places faster going places alone. And, except for Hal and his family, I traveled alone.

Anyway I feel for Jenny like a tree with an axe in its belly crashes to the ground. I loved her so damn much I didn't know what end was up. There's a terrible pain that goes with a love like I had for that woman. Suddenly you're face-to-face with your own mortality. Sure I had all that money. Sure I had all that power. I was big cheese in those parts. But all I could think about was how many years I had ahead of me. How many years I'd have with Jenny. And I resented every empty year that went before. I'd trade very one of them in-and all that money and power, too-for my lost young years.

The love didn't cease even when I found out what she was. You can forgive a love like that anything. Well, almost anything. I couldn't forgive her, nor can I ever forgive her Hal.

Somehow in spite of all the love-sickness I got the plant built and operating. It'd be the biggest lumber distribution center in the Northwest. Owen sat behind an executive's desk in a private office and twiddled his thumbs all day. Jenny, as much as anyone else, helped me pull it all together. Hal came down once in awhile but there was a tension there I didn't understand. I thought it was Hal, so I never asked him down again. I'll say that for Jen, she has a mind for business. Probably got that place running like a little gold watch. Owen may be in the office but you can bet Jenny runs the place. If Fisher Enterprises is still in business you can be certain it's Jenny who's pulling the strings. Together we built the house.

What a place! The show place of seven counties. We could see three mountains, Hood, Helens, and Rainier, out our living room windows. The driveway alone, up to the house, cost more than any other construction in town including the bank and the school. This amused Jenny. How she loved being driven up that road and through that town in her big black car. She was vain, I had to admit that, but that only made me prouder of her. I got her a real chauffer, uniform and all.

Our wedding was the biggest event that happened that year for miles around. We even made the Portland and Vancouver society pages. Jenny was proud of that. She wore the wedding gown she'd worn at her first wedding and it fit her like she'd had it made the week before. My God I was proud.

When she turned this big gold eyes on me I would have died for her. I'd have given her anything on earth. I did give her everything I could think of, but for Jenny that wasn't enough. She played another game.

I began to suspect something was not quite right about three years after we married. It had nothing to do with her; she was all butter and icing. What changed was me. There was something wrong with me. I was sick all the time. Nothing sat right on my stomach. I ached and pained everywhere. My head hurt. It didn't seem as though it was working half the time. I was punchy and I knew it. And I fought it. Jenny was the picture of health. She seemed to get younger and healthier the sicker I became. She was also the soul of consideration. She was an angel. A saint. She nursed me, fussed over me, served me special meals she'd prepared with her own hands," Jasper made a face. "She never left my side. I could believe every word I'd heard about her saintly qualities.

Well, now, I'm a mighty tough old lumberjack. Or I was. Never been sick a day in my life. Had the constitution of a grizzly bear. My Dad lived to be ninety-eight. Died in his sleep. My Mom out-lived him a year. I wasn't about to give up the ghost at sixty-eight.

I never complained. I didn't want to fret or worry my bride," he made another face. "Before it was over she must have felt she trying to kill a grizzly bear with a butter knife. And I'm a proud man, too, or was, and when my ails and ailments and dizzy spells and fits really began getting the best of me, using the business as an excuse, I slipped away to the Mayo. They found enough arsenic in my system to kill a herd of mountain goats. Lucky I got there when I did.

Even then I didn't suspect Jenny. I thought it must be something in the house, the plaster or the paint or something else that was doing it to me. Just about that time Boots showed up.

Remember him, my driver? Well, when Hal, he'd been working for him, told him I was sick, Boots tracked me down.

'Boss', he said the minute he saw me, 'she's giving you the shaft.'

'That's a terrible thing to say, Boots.'

'Listen, man, you outta see yourself. I never saw a man go downhill so fast. Hal said the last time he saw you, you looked like walking death. And you do. And that's what you are sure enough. It sure as hell ain't the climate in those parts. What's she doin', slippin' a little rat poison in your soup?'

Leave it to Boots to hit the nail on the head first swing at it. That soup line was too close for comfort. Jenny was famous for her homemade soup. If I'd let her, she would have served me soup for breakfast.

'But why, Boots? I love the woman, I'd give, I've given, her everything.'

'Some women want something else out of life, Boss, and she's one of those. I had her spotted from the first. Tildy, too. She wanted me to tell you and I should've.'

I still didn't believe him, but, as I said, I was a cautious man and I respected his insight. Anyway I went back soon as I was strong enough and hired a detective."

"Jesus," David said.

"Adams," I said. "It can't be?"

Jasper look up still lost in his story, he was a good storyteller, his eyes were far away, "I believe the name was Adams. Goodman Adams as I recall. It's been a long time."

"Alias Ace."

"Ace? I don't know about that. Anyway the man got the goods on Jenny and her wretched daughter and son-in-law, to. All the information I gave you came right out of his files. He poured the entire story out to me in his office one bleak wintry day."

"So you ran?"

"Like hell I ran."

And for a brief moment we caught a glimpse of the old Jasper Johns. "I stood and fought. To tell you the truth, though, this man Adams suggested I run. 'She owns the whole damn county, Fish. If you value your life you'll get out while the getting's good. Money isn't everything you know.'

I turned and left his office. The first thing I did was find a phone and call Hal."

Jasper paused for a long time and ran his hand across his forehead. "Terrible day. One of the most terrible days of my life. I don't think I'll ever forget it. The person in the Vancouver office didn't recognize my voice and that was odd, they all knew me. 'Let me speak to Barlow.' I said. 'Who's this? The voice asked. 'This is Fisher! Damn it!' I was mad and taking it out on anybody. 'Mr. Fisher! You haven't heard?' 'Heard what? Man, spit it out.' 'Mr. Barlow is dead. He died in his sleep last night. The whole office is in turmoil. I thought everyone knew by now.'

I couldn't believe what I was hearing. I dropped the phone back on the hook. But before I did I heard the voice again, distinctly. 'Jhon-vieve sends her love, Fish.'

I got out of Portland that day. Rented a car, didn't risk going to the airport and drove straight through to Frisco didn't even stop to eat. I still had some money. My personal checking account had several thousand dollars in it. I could get around. For a while. At least until I figured out what to do. Like all rich men, I had rich friends. I called an old Aussie buddy who was building a boat in Kowloon, it seemed a nice safe distance, and as soon as I could arrange it I left for Hong Kong.

My spirits were as low as a snake. I'd been responsible for my best friend's death. But those crazy Aussie's could revive the dead. I spent the next six months helping Cluny with the boat. I was a big help to him, too. I know wood, so I paid my way, and then we set sail on the Witchery, that's what he decided to name her, after Jenny. It was a good year I forgot my troubles in every bar from the Tasman Sea to Molokai. Had good times, actually. I was taking a well-deserved vacation. My first, if the truth were known. Getting my health back. The Aussies thought the whole thing was a gas. My being sick, I mean it was a running joke on the boat. 'Hey'mite,' they'd yell when I'd come up on deck, 'ad yur rat poison for the die?'

We were beginning to formulate a plan. After all, we figured, all we had to do was get rid of the woman and take the company back. My friends could hardly wait. They had a barrel of imaginative suggestions as to what we ought to do with Jenny. On dull watches the game, 'who gets Jenny tonight mite?' that rough and tumble crew could hardly wait to tangle with her and the whole damn town. I'd move back in the house on the hill with an army of roughnecks who'd by God teach Jenny and her kin a thing or two. But first we had to win a Transpac.

That was the fatal error. We sailed to L.A., a new boat, the prettiest hull in the fleet that year. Made a big splash. Pictures in all the sailing magazines, newspapers, tabloids. Even made Playboy. Beauties from everywhere, not in the least shy about shedding their clothes, swarmed all over the boat. Guess somebody caught a shot of me at the same time. I'll never know.

We were sliding down to Oahu that big fire-engine red spinnaker up and going like sixty. We were ahead of the pack and still moving out. There were eight of us on board. Six crew members, the skipper-navigator, and the cook.

Now I'd known Bobby since before I came aboard. Big bugger. Tough as only an Aussie can be tough. He was a good kid. We were about half way across and Bobby and me had the midnight watch. I was getting up to go down below and get us a cup of hot coffee when they blew. Dolphin. Everywhere. Well, every sailor loves the dolphins. Bobby jumped up laughing and ran to the rail. I was right behind him. The good old Witchery was sailing herself. The next thing I knew I was over the side.

I wasn't worried. Bobby was right there. He reached down to give me a hand up, I grasped it. I actually had his hand in mine, sometimes I can still feel it, when he hit me. As I blacked out and floated off I heard him call softly after me, 'Jhon-vieve send'er love, mite.'

I woke up on board a Japanese fishing boat. I'll never know how."

Lorraine, who'd slipped quietly back in the house with an enormous platter of chocolate cake in her hand, whispered, "The dolphins knows," and looked stricken with awe.

"Perhaps. At any rate I spent the next three weeks on board the vessel. No one spoke a word of English. Somebody gave me an old violin they had on board and I learned to play.

They were a swell bunch of guys I can tell you. But they couldn't help me, I had too much time to think. Oh, I helped them when I could. Man, do those men work! Backbreaking work when you're working. The doldrums when you're not. Well, I guess I was in my own state of the doldrums. They were everywhere. Once my new friends had to tie me down to keep me from jumping over the side. I was convinced Jenny was on board. I had no friends. No money. I had no future. I had no past. I didn't even have a name. When we got to Honolulu the crew gave me the violin and two hundred bucks. They all chipped in for me and that's when Gypsy Jake was born. A couple of the crew members got me to the Salvation Army store where I bought some clothes and a cheap cardboard suitcase and here I am. I got right off that boat and on an inter-island flight to Kauai and I've been here ever since. Don't even ask how long that is. I've not kept track of time. Not so sure I want to know either. Time lost is gone forever.

That's about ends it. I'd almost forgotten what the whole thing was all about until the day I heard you speak her name over the phone."

"The day Alex went lame," I exclaimed. "Of course. I remember now."

"It all came back and I figured she'd found me again. So I ran. Being Gypsy Jake wasn't all bad. I was alive anyway and I could trust again."

"He ran my place," Lorraine said.

"Yes, to Lorraine. Now, I'm not a drinking man, never was, but I've been on a toot ever since. I drank the New Papeete dry and I guess I told Lorraine everything."

"He made me promise no to tell."

"I've been drunk ever since. Lorraine found me again, don't ask me how, drying out in that horrible place on the hill. My God those poor people." Lorraine nodded.

"Last night Lorraine insisted I tell you everything. She walked me up and down those hospital corridors until some sense returned and she told me all about you folks and your father. She said it was a matter of life or death. She gave me no peace."

Lorraine grinned again.

'I think I've done the right thing," He looked up at us. "If I can help you and your dad, I'll do it. I can't run and I can't hide forever. A man can only be pushed so far and I've been pushed so far I've come up on the other side."

"Good man," David said.

"I'm so proud of you, Jasper."

"Better he come home with me," Lorraine said.

"No. Better he stay with us."

"He'ave to eat those cookies? I gots cake."

"Okay, but he's going to eat the cookies, too." I gave him some more juice, a thick sandwich, and made him promise to get a good night's sleep.

Lorraine went home.

David and I climbed the stairway to bed and fell asleep exhausted. And that's how we left it until morning.

Charlie

The next morning David and I, with Jasper's help, devised a plan of action. I, of course, had already consulted my oracle, just as David had consulted his. This time the instructions were clear, Father must come to Hawaii.

I threw Ta Ch'u with no moving lines. 'It is a favorable time for crossing the great sea', it said. I was particularly taken with this piece of advice, 'Good fortune results from not eating at home.'

My god, you don't suppose she was brewing him soup already?

"But how are we going to get him here?" I asked David.

He shook his head.

"The wedding's a week away. We've already received the invitation. As, so it seemed, had everybody else in town.

"Tell him Karen's sick," Jasper said, and David and I turned in surprise.

"Of course," David said.

Jasper nodded. "Tell Hal a kid was sick and all the Fisher lumber on all the West Coast docks could rot as far as he cared. Your dad sounds a lot like Hal, Karen."

David and I just looked at each other.

"Lorraine says he's a fine upstanding man," Jasper continued, "I can't wait to meet him."

I nodded.

"Try it," I said. "But please don't get him so upset he has a heart attack. Play it down. Keep it low. But get him here."

"I think it'll work," Jasper said.

"Okay, David, you call."

Before David got a chance to call, the phone rang. It was Lorraine. She's a trip to talk to on the phone, but I gathered, just barely, that a waterfall, the wind, the trees, and all the stars in the sky and the moon, too, had told her the Colonel was to 'come Hawaii'.

*

David called from his office. I listened in on the bedroom extension. Jasper was stationed at the kitchen phone only because we didn't want him to feel left out. It was, to me at least, a most gratifying conversation. It's not often a daughter gets to hear her father so distraught over the state of her health. It was something, I suppose, like reading your own obituary. When it's a good review.

"She can't be sick. She's never been sick a day in her entire life. What do they think is wrong?"

"They don't know, Charlie. It's really got them stumped." David tried to distract him.

"They don't know? What kind of half-baked medicine men do you have on that backwoods island anyhow? You know I never approved of you kids moving way out there. I told you you'd get sick or something and there'd be nobody around to help. I'll call Mayo. I'll send Jenny."

If he hadn't been so upset, he'd have heard three distinct gasps.

I peeked down the stairs to see how Jasper was doing. He seemed to be holding up. A bit pale perhaps, but he hadn't dropped the phone. Yet.

"She doesn't need a doctor right now, Charlie. She needs you. Desperately. I know if you were to come over it would help. It may be emotional."

"You mean she's sick in the head?"

I put my hand over the mouthpiece and giggled.

"Karen is very level-headed."

"Then what do you mean? Why are you being so vague and mysterious? You've always been able to express yourself clearly. Why the confusion now?"

"I'm not being mysterious or vague. Nor am I confused, Charlie. Puzzled, of course. All the people involved in this are puzzled. That's why we need you," David said. Afterwards he said he wished he'd looked up some symptoms, but he did the best he could under the circumstances. "It's probably nothing but some silly female complaint She's nearly fifty, you know. She has these aches and pains. Cramps."

I groaned.

"Headaches. Backaches. She's a mess, Charlie. Hurts everywhere. She's running a fever and her feet hurt." David continued to extemporize. I think he had me confused with the horses.

"How high a fever?" Father asked.

"About a hundred and five, " David said vaguely. He is an engineer not a doctor.

"A hundred and five," Father bawled.

"A hundred and six?" David tried again.

"When did you take it last? How fast is it rising? Get that girl cooled off. Now. Cold packs. Wet sheets. My mother always used to use wet sheets. Listen, David, if you don't get that temperature broke she can go just like that!" We could hear his fingers snap. "Or else she'll start to hallucinate. She'll see snakes and lizards or something. Why do her feet hurt? Get her off her feet. Can't you yokels even do a simple thing like that? Get her feet in the air."

In spite of himself David was intrigued. "In the air? You mean like on a pulley?" David asked. "Traction! That's it! You see, Charlie, just talking to you helps. Imagine what you could do if you were here. She needs traction. She's got a splintered disc."

I put my hand of the phone and groaned again.

"My God, man! Get her in traction. Now!"

"Well, she fights it. If you can get over here I know you'll be able to calm her down and get her to listen to reason. You know how flighty she is. She just doesn't like the sound of traction."

Father snorted, "Today, David, in all modern and well-equipped hospitals, they have silent traction. It's absolutely absurd in this day and age to have to put up with noisy traction."

"We have silent traction here, too, Charlie, but you know how she hates and fears hospitals. Remember the awful time we had getting her to the hospital when Alice was born."

I remembered. Mother had to hold Father up. He was falling down, he was in such distress. I was in labor. At the hospital the nurses had to revive him. Father got a room and a bed before I did.

David was still rattling on about traction machines. That was more his line. "Home traction machines are pretty primitive, Charlie and noisy," he said. "It's just part of the over all problem."

"Keeps her awake at night?"

"Yeah, that's it. She suffers from terrible insomnia. Hasn't slept a wink in weeks."

"David you're an engineer, oil the damn thing. The poor little tyke has got to get her sleep if she's going to get better. Oh, how well I know the healing power of sleep."

"And she'll sleep so much better, like a baby, in fact, as soon as you get here. She needs some hand-holding."

"Hold her hand, David, Oh, son, hold her little hand. If I'd only been there when her mother died to hold her hand. How I torture myself thinking about it."

"You were always much better at handholding than me," David said quickly.

"Can she come to the phone?"

"No," David said, "the traction machine won't reach that far."

"Poor child. Poor little girl. Get me tickets. Get me out of here tonight. I don't know how, but do it. I won't take no for an answer. Let that poor little baby get a good night's sleep and she'll be fine. I know it! When she was little girl, David, I used to sing her to sleep."

"That'll do it, Charlie. When you get here you can sing her to sleep every night."

"She used to love cowboy songs. I knew all the words to all the latest cowboy songs. Learned them from listening to the radio. Try some good old cowboy songs, boy. 'Come along boys and listen to my tale and I'll tell you a story 'bout the old Chisholm Trail, Come a kiyi yippy yippy yi yippy yay come a'kiyi yippy yippy yay!"

"Hey, Charlie, if she could only hear that she'd be up and dancing around in no time. I'll get the tickets. You get packed and out to the airport. The tickets will be waiting for you at the counter. See you tomorrow. Practice that song."

"You sure you don't want me to bring Jenny?"

David thought fast. "I know Karen wouldn't want to meet your new bride, her new mother," he said it, he really did, "while she's under the weather. You know how vain she is."

"Very well, David, son, for god's sake get that temperature down. Aspirin. Lots of aspirin. A buffered aspirin the kind you see advertised on television all the time. Gets right to the problem. And get her feet in the air. That's an order!"

"Sure thing, Charlie. Right away."

When Father hung up I said, "David that was the most ridiculous conversation I've ever heard. Cramps for god's sake."

"What did you expect? I don't know anything about sick people. Nobody ever gets sick around here. Anyway he bought it, he's coming and that's all that matters."

"What's a traction machine, David?"

"It's a thing that gets your feet in the air," David said. "Sounds like fun. I think I'll try to put one together."

"Make sure it doesn't squeak."

"I'll design an oil can to go with it."

Downstairs, his ears a little red, Jasper tiptoed back to his nook in the living room. Poor old man, I thought, what an introduction to
Father.

*.

This next is David's story, so I'll just let him tell it. He tells it often. He elaborates and embellishes but he says more of it is true than you might believe...

We talked it over and I decided Karen and Jasper should stay home. I'd meet Charlie at the airport. By myself.

We'd spring our surprises on him at the house. Charlie can be a bitch to handle in a crowd.

I drove Karen's utility wagon. It wouldn't suit Charlie's style but maybe it was big enough to hold his stuff. I was wrong about that, but it didn't matter.

Just outside the town there was a two-car accident. It must have happened minutes before I got there, things were still flaky. A '76 pickup loaded with baled hay and an old International flatbed carrying a load of crated chicken had collided head-on at a narrow bend in the road.

No one was hurt. The trucks were both lying on their sides, wheels spinning, and bales of hay and crates of chickens were spilled out all over the road. The drivers of the vehicles, farming-types from the outback, stood in the middle of the road shaking their fists and swearing at each other while a whole bloody army of goddam chickens, clucking and flapping, dropped feathers and chicken shit all over everything.

Guys around me were jumping out of their cars to chase them.

One cocky old son-of-a-bitch with a comb as red as a baboon's ass stretched his neck and crowed his last.

A fat old haole broad in a nurse's uniform grabbed him from behind and tossed him head first in the trunk of her Buick.

The highway was blocked in all the lanes with trucks and bales of hay. Chickens, with people hot on their ass, were running every which way. One squawking old hen landed on the hood of the wagon and I blasted her off with the horn. Someone caught her on the next bounce.

It sure as hell was a sight to see. If I hadn't had a plane to meet I'd have enjoyed it more. People and chickens were running in all directions. Two kids got in a fight over a scrawny old bird and damn near pulled the thing apart. It laid an egg right on the highway and it didn't even break. Which made everybody laugh. No one was really mad. Except the owner of the flatbed. He was tearing around like one of his chickens trying to be everywhere at once.

'"You leave my chickens be," he shouted at the wind, but no one paid any attention to him. Cops, who finally showed up to get traffic moving again, drove off with a pair of chickens in the back of their blue sedan.

"Chicken thieves," I hollered. "I got your number."

They flipped me the bird.

By the time I got the hell out of there Charlie's jet had come and gone and another one had landed. We were close enough to the airport to hear the first one land. And take off. They don't stick around long in this neck of the woods.

I figured Charlie'd been cooling his heels for forty-five minutes or so and steeled myself for a lecture. I liked the old man, don't get me wrong, but he can be a royal pain in the ass. I figured he'd be mad as hell but again I was wrong. Charlie wasn't mad, but everybody else was.

All I could see when I turned the corner into the airport road were stalled cars. Hoods were up. Radiators were steaming. Guys were cussing and swearing and turning red in the face.

Cars entering the road were at a standstill. They were backed up ahead of me all the way to the main entrance and behind me they were beginning to back up on the highway.

No one was leaving either, although the out-going lane was clear.

Whatever was going on up there must be good.

I pulled the car over onto the shoulder. Parked it. Got out. Locked the door, and set out walking. Charlie might buy one accident, but damned if he'd buy two.

The road ahead and behind me was beginning to look like Columbus, Ohio, the day the dam broke. At least half a hundred people were trudging up the road hauling suitcases. I was lucky there, at least, I had no luggage and I hadn't far to go. The old man and I could grab a couple of cool ones in the bar while we waited for the mess to clear. If I knew him the two of us together wouldn't be able to haul all his luggage back to the car if we made three trips.

And I had a bloody good idea who'd be making the trips alone.

Whatever was holding up the parade had taken place right in front of the terminal building. As I got closer I could see a group of Japanese tourists bailing out of an air-conditioned tour bus. This pig, I hate the goddam smelly things, was parked in one of the narrow lanes right in front of the building. In front of it, in the other lane, was a wide-bodied orange and white ambulance. Its yellow lights were slowly turning and it was making a noise like a bull elephant in rut.

I guess it was waiting for an incoming passenger.

Jesus Christ! Charlie!

I began to run. All the parking spaces in front of the terminal were full. That was a five minute loading zone and unloading zone, the cops carry stop watches, and that big mother of an ambulance, parked illegally in front of the main door, right in everybody's way, was too wide to let the bus pass.

The driver of the bus stood in the middle of the street and with his hat shooed those dippy little tourist-types out the door. A flock of those camera-toters surged around in front of the ambulance gawking and staring and snapping pictures. They'd have to get home and look at their photos to find out where the hell they'd been. A helpful baggage attendant from inside the terminal was tossing luggage out of the bus and piling it up in the street in front of the ambulance.

Also, in front of the ambulance, behind the bus, a fight was starting. Two cars locked bumper-to-bumper and caved in broadside would probably keep that lane blocked for the next couple of hours. These three drivers, two burly locals in work-clothes, and what looked like a Japanese Sumo wrestler in a business suit, were standing in the street shouting at each other.

This potential riot was moving out of the cuss word, fist shaking stage, into a real knockdown drag out.

I gave these guys plenty of room and crossed the street in the pedestrian lane with all those bustling Japanese.

A rent-a-cop, mad as hell at the bus driver's maneuvering, was turning the air purple and blowing his whistle. He was so mad he was jumping up and down. The driver took it for a while and then started shouting back. "Lis'sen Mac," he yelled and he sounded like he came right out of the Bronx, "My job's to get these little nippers on that plane and off this bus. I can't fly them to Oahu. I can't put'em up at my house. If they miss that plane I won't have a house. If they miss that plane I lose my job and who'll pay the rent. You? I don't care how many dead and dyin' you got to get outta here in that thing." He waved at the ambulance. "I gotta get these guys outta here."

I think they put cops around here in blue serge suits just to make them mean. In this heat they must itch like hell.

"There's a lot of other guys that got a plane to catch, bud." The cop pointed his finger at cars lined up for blocks behind the bus. "I got a job to do, too."

Some young haole chick stuck her head out a car window and yelled, "Fuck your jobs. I want to go home."

"You tell'em sistah," somebody yelled back.

"Move that pile of shit. I got to catch a plane. You want my wife to divorce me?" The blonde sitting in the seat alongside the guy grinned and waved.

"I wish I had your problem, buddy," another guy yelled. "My old lady wouldn't divorce me if I had ten blondes in the front seat."

"You move it!" The ambulance driver threw his key away in a direction other than the three-man bawl going on behind the bus. I didn't blame him

A beat up old Chevy sedan full of surfers, with boards, each guy with a chicken tucked under his arm, spun around the corner in the wrong lane and screeched to a halt in front of the bus. Everyone jumped out, chickens and all. They were busy for a minute unloading their boards and then they split for the terminal. They were gone and out of there in two minutes. When the cop found his voice again and screamed, a couple of the kids dropped their chickens.

There were still some chickens inside the car that somebody couldn't figure out a way to carry, I guess, and these flapped out the window. The cop was yelling himself hoarse and all those goddam chickens were running around shitting and squawking.

Some guy in a Ford pick-up watching the surfer's maneuver got the same idea. He screeched in behind the sedan and took off running for the terminal this guy acted like he was headed for the can. When he opened his doors and leaped out, twelve empty pop-top cans of beer fell in the street.

The apoplectic cop, at a flat-out run, threw his body into the lanes the ambulance was in and saved the day. For me anyway. There was no stopping the floodwater of cars pulling in front of the bus. There were about eight of them. Some of these guys didn't even bother closing their doors, they were out and gone so fast. You can bet these were rented cars.

Guys inside the terminal were pouring into the street now. I don't know who was manning the ticket desk. Ticket-takers in their aloha shirts were milling and gawking right along with the rest of the mob. And it was a mob. Just the right size for a riot.

Fry cooks in grease-smudged aprons stood in a clump by the cafeteria door.

Drunks, drinks in hand, airport regulars, poured out of the bar. These guys, blinking in the light of day, were spoiling for a fight.

When the men in the bumper-locked, fender-bent cars started swinging, they had plenty of company.

Inside a voice on the intercom pleaded with passengers to board their flights. The voice repeated the message in nervous Japanese.

He could have saved his breath. None of the Japanese tourists was going anywhere. They were to busy taking pictures.

Of Charlie.

Charlie, in a brown suede cowboy suit with fringe on the sleeves, was the only calm person in the whole damn county as far I could tell.

He was rocking back and forth on his heels, his big black Stetson pushed to the back of his head, his long white wig flying, smiling broadly at his fans.

The more the flash bulbs popped, the more he hammed it up. When he saw me he waved an imperious hand, "David, son, it's about time. Good to see you. This is my son-in-law, David," he introduced me to the crowd. "Late as usual. He live your island." He tried a bit of pidgin and threw me an all-forgiving grin. "Where's the car?"

About two miles back," I yelled over the din. "What's going on around here anyway? We'll have to carry your bags or wait in the bar for the all clear."

"Nonsense, David, my boy. I'll have the driver load them in the back of the ambulance." He gestured behind him to a pile of luggage.

"Sure if you can get them to do that, Charlie, but I imagine they have better things to do with their ambulance."

It was a relief to know it wasn't waiting for him. He looked bright and chipper. His voice, which is big as all outdoors, carried through the crowd.

"What could be more important than my daughter?" he asked.

"What's Karen got to do with this?"

"Well, now, my boy, we can't very well drive her to the hospital in a bumpy old pickup truck can we? By the time we got here she'd be in pieces."

"That's your ambulance?"

"It isn't mine, David. Of course it isn't mine. Why would I want an ambulance? Actually I don't know that private parties can own an ambulance." He beckoned the ambulance driver over. "Tell me, my man, he said, "can I buy an ambulance?"

The driver was speechless.

"Not that I want to buy one you understand. It just poses an interesting question. David, David is my son-in-law," he introduced me to the driver, "always poses interesting questions. Keeps an old man on his toes I can tell you. David's very intelligent. My daughter, too, of course. Still I never heard of anyone who owned his own ambulance. Did you?"

The driver's mouth was open, but no sound was coming out. When he shook his head his jaw waggled.

"Sounds like a rather impractical purchase. How often would you use the thing, eh, David, how often?"

The driver continued to nod.

"No, David, it isn't mine. I just…"

"You just what, Charlie?"

"One moment, David. Hold on. Son," he pointed at the driver, "pick up those keys. It is just not seemly for an adult male to act like a child. You listen to an old man who was a man when men were men," he drew a breath and expanded his chest a quarter of an inch. Then he coughed. "I'm going on eighty," he said, which wasn't true and was apropos of nothing. "Put my bags in the back. When we pick up my daughter we'll unload them." He waved in the general direction of the luggage on the sidewalk.

Charlie's performance was attracting as much attention as the fight. A little girl, about three years old, got away from her mother, ran out in the street and threw her arms around Charlie's legs. She must have mistaken him for Colonel Saunders. There was a faint resemblance. She looked up at him with total adoration. Charlie reached down, picked her up, gave her a big kiss and patted her bottom. "Now who belongs to this little doll. Speak up. Quick. Or I'll take her home with me."

The kid's mother, an enormous local girl darted forth, grabbed the kid, giggled and ran back in to the crowd. Charlie beamed.

The ambulance driver, who, by now, could not have told you his name if his life depended on it-Charlie has his own brainwashing techniques-did as Charlie ordered and began to load luggage.

"Charlie we don't need an ambulance."

"Of course we do, David. I'm surprised you haven't taken Karen to the hospital long before this. You're behaving in a very irresponsible manner, son. It isn't like you. And she is my favorite daughter."

Too bad Karen wasn't here to hear that. I knew it would have pepped her up.

"Jenny says a splintered disc is absolutely the worst kind of spinal injury. That poor child, unless we are very careful, can end up in a wheelchair. For the rest of her life. Think of that David. No. No. We must get her to a place where she can receive professional attention. She may have to come back to the states with me. That is, of course, as soon as she's strong enough to travel. We must get that girl on her feet in time for the wedding. Can't get married without my favorite daughter being there now can I?

Jenny says in the states they make these spiffy little Barbarella braces, all stainless steel and white leather. Just special for cases like this. So she can be up and around you know. For a little while anyway. On special occasions such as weddings and such she'll be able to move around. Otherwise it's flat on her back."

I had to think. But it's impossible to think when Charlie's around. Charlie should be flat on his back. My head was spinning. What in the hell was I going to do, throw him over my shoulder and physically haul him out of here? The crowd would lynch me.

He was posing again.

Bowing. Smiling. Waving his hat. Who the hell did he think he was for Chris' sakes, Robert Redford?

Just as I was about to grab him anyway, a goofy-looking character marched sternly out of the terminal building. He headed straight for us.

"I want to know what's going on around here!" That was crazy, all he had to do was look around, a riot was going on around here. Charlie had arrived.

Charlie ignored him. No one spoke to Charlie in that tone of voice.

"Get that ambulance out of here. No one called for an ambulance."

Charlie pushed his hat back on his head and put his hands on his hips. He spread his legs far apart and pivoted to face the man. "There you are mistaken, my good man, I, yes, indeed, I, Colonel Charles Warren Skinner. The third. Ordered the ambulance. My father, Charles Warren Skinner, Junior, was a very famous Indian fighter. His father, Charles Warren Skinner, Senior, was a General in the Union Army."

This was ridiculous. Charlie's grandfather's name was Fergus and he came right out of the Highland painted blue.

"I ordered the ambulance," he continued, "and here, in fact, if you have eyes in your head, it is! It's for my daughter, Karen, if you must know."

And then Charlie pulled on of those sudden, inexplicable about-faces for which he's famous. "My dear man," he purred, the kind of a purr a man-eating tiger purrs just before it snaps a fellow's head off, "I can't believe it. Do you by any chance have relatives in the Pacific Northwest?"

The hulk looked stunned.

"Pah, pah, Pacific…" he stuttered.

"Pacific Northwest," Charlie enunciated very slowly. "That's right. In the states?" Charlie still hadn't caught on that Hawaii was a state. "West Coast. Up North?" He pointed his finger at the sky and shook it. He gave me a look that said plainly, where do you get these idiots? "Your resemblance to my son-in-law, well not my son-in-law, my son-in-law to be, David is my son-in-law, but my son-in-law to be, I'm not yet married to his mother-in-law, how confusing relationships are, aren't they? David, look at the man. He looks exactly like Owen."

The last thing in the world I wanted to do was look at the man. I hoped he wasn't taking too good a look at me, either. All I wanted was to get Charlie out of here before someone was smart enough to figure out that he was cause of this mess and tear him limb from limb. The trouble with that was nobody would tear Charlie limb for limb, but they might start with an innocent guy who looked like maybe he was with the guy who started the trouble.

Off in a distance I could hear a police siren. The cops were on the way. It had taken them long enough. They'd probably had to go home and pen up all those chicken.

All I needed was the cops!

The noise by now was at rock concert level. Horns blared. Voices rose. People swore. The loud speaker inside the terminal was still squawking.

As were the chickens. Someone had turned his radio up full blast. Some discordant, raucous, rock group serenaded the whole damn nut house.

All the while flash bulbs popped and Charlie posed.

He also continued his monologue.

"The Fisher-Woodbury's are a fine old family. Well known in their part of the country. The Pacific Northwest you know. Very old name. Very old family. You could be Owen's twin brother. Identical twin, David they could be identical twins."

The poor bastard who looked like Owen, as if that weren't bad enough, looked as confused as a pole-axed ox.

"You do seem to have some sort of traffic problem around here," Charlie ventured conversationally. "Perhaps my son-in-law, David Ho…"

"…Ho! Stop! That's it Charlie. We must get to Karen." It was the act of a desperate man, all the cops had to do was find out David Holt was in the vicinity. "That's right! She's got to get to the hospital. Every second counts. Tell that guy to get this baby in gear and let's get the hell out of here."

I began to shove tourists out of the way, clearing a path for the ambulance.

"Emergency! Emergency!" I shouted which was stupid. None of these people spoke English. Anyhow I managed to shove Charlie into the back of the ambulance and slam the doors, He was discussing my talents at unraveling traffic jams, designing highway systems and under and over passes, too. When I slammed the door on him I heard him say, "David! They picked up all the wrong luggage."

"Shut up Charlie," I said and hoped the door was locked. I grabbed the ambulance driver and his partner and managed to shove all three of us into the cab. "Get out of here. Quick!" I yelled and we backed out of there, siren moaning, yellow lights turning and flashing, the only vehicle for miles around that could move, and out onto the road where we turned around. We drove out as the cops drove in.

I ducked.

The ambulance driver waved. The cops didn't pay any attention to us. We were legit. More cops were coming down the road. It looked like a cop convention. We dodged them. I don't suppose any of us knew who had the right of way.

I jumped out of the cab when we reached Karen's car, turned on the ignition, the motor purred, spun around and led the ambulance home.

I could see Charlie's head in the cab behind me. He'd jumped out of the back when I jumped out of the front and was sitting, Stetson and all, waving his arms like a cavalry officer motioning his men to charge, with the driver and his buddy.

His jaw never stopped wagging.

As soon as I calmed down I thought, why in the hell don't we let him marry that woman? He'd drive her crazy long before she could poison him.

The Geriatric Gang

David should have been home two hours ago; I was beginning to worry. Jasper, who'd been seated in the kitchen counter, sensing my concern, began to pace. He looked very much the successful businessman in clothes Lorraine had borrowed.

"It's okay, Jasper, " I said, "the flight was probably delayed or they ran into traffic. If there was anything wrong David would call."

"I'm nervous," Jasper said tugging at his collar. "I've heard so much about your father. Grand old man. And you know I haven't been myself for quite some time."

"You have nothing to worry about, " I said, "I know you'll be fine. You and Father are going to get along famously. He can't help but be grateful for what you have to tell him."

"I doubt that," Jasper said. "No man likes to be told a woman is making a fool of him."

"Better he find out now." I said.

The sound of the car approaching cut our conversation short. "There they are. You ready? Don't be nervous."

Jasper nodded and walked over to a chair by the fire. I started back upstairs to bed. The muu I wore was as young and innocent as a child's. I patted my lace and ruffles and tossed my hair, which was tied with a big black bow and hung down my back. I not only felt nervous, I felt silly. We had prepared a dramatic scenario, but I was uncomfortable in the role. I hoped David and Jasper could handle theirs.

When I looked out the window and saw the ambulance, I panicked, all plans forgotten. "God." I cried, and ruining everything, ran back down the stairs and out the door. David, when he saw me, motioned me into the house.

"Go back inside," he shouted.

"What happened? Where's Father?"

"Get in the house!" David yelled.

I was convinced that Father had had a heart attack on the plane and they'd driven him here in the ambulance so we could say good-bye. When Father, in the front of the ambulance, caught sight of me running towards him, he opened the door and began to descend, awkwardly, back-end first.

"Karen," he yelled.

"Be careful," I yelled back.

He missed the narrow running board and fell on his duff. I ran to his side and threw myself on the ground alongside him.

"Are you all right?"

"Fine sweetheart. Just give me a hand up. No! Don't give me a hand up!"

He snatched his hand away! I thought he was having another attack.

The two men who'd been in the cab with him clambered out the other side. "That her?" one man asked. "Looks okay to me."

"Some times they do," the other man said.

"What are you doing out of bed? Get that stretcher, man, quickly. We must get her off her feet. Jenny says the worst thing for her to be is on her feet."

The attendant ran to the rear of the vehicle and began tossing out luggage.

"Wait. Gentlemen!" David, meanwhile, had jumped put of my car and ran to the back of the ambulance, too. He began tossing luggage in. "This has been a terrible mistake. We don't need an ambulance here. You can see the lady is fine."

"The Colonel said she fell off a horse," One of men said. He gave David a dirty look and began to toss the luggage David had just tossed in, back out again.

"Probably in shock," the other man said. Every time one of the men tossed a piece of luggage out, David tossed it back in.

"He said it was all his fault. I thought that nice old guy was gonna cry. She wanted to take piano lessons but he wanted her to learn to ride a horse. You see he kinda wanted a boy. And she was just a mite of a little girl scared to death of horses. If he hadn't forced her on that horse the first time she'd never have fallen off and broke her back."

I was in shock. "Father how could you?"

David and the men were still tossing luggage in and out, but David was losing. There were two of them and they were motivated.

"I had to tell them something, Karen, it was an emergency."

"I haven't fallen off a horse in years."

"Some guys fall off piano benches. I heard of one guy who was in traction for six months from falling off a piano bench."

"He says he's going to shoot that horse. Right between the headlights."

"Look," David pleaded, "my father-in-law has a vivid imagination. She didn't fall off a horse."

"I never wanted to take piano lessons in my life. I hated piano lessons."

"If you'd stuck to your piano, lady, you wouldn't be in the shape you're in today."

That damn muu. "...And no one is going to shoot my horse."

"I will shoot that beast! I will shoot any ornery hoss that hurts my daughter so sorely," Father turned to the ambulance attendant. "That's right where we shoot them, son. Right between the eyes. Bang! Bang!" He pointed his fingers and aimed.

"Father I'm not hurt! Sorely or otherwise. I am not hurt at all. David do what you can with those men, I'll get him to the house." Together we struggled to rise.

The ambulance attendants, having finally won the battle of the bags, removed a folded-up stretcher and started after me. David tried to interfere, but he was shoved aside. These were big men. They also looked as though they meant business.

I picked up my skirts and sprinted for the house. It's almost impossible to run in a long skirt.

Father was still trying to put himself together. "Get her, men! Don't let her injure herself again. She'll be in two pieces."

"Stop!" David yelled and tried a tackle. He might as well have tried to tackle Alex. The man shook his leg and David was on the ground empty handed.

"Look, man, we drove all the way out here to pick up a injured lady and take her back to the hospital and that's what we're gonna do." Both of the attendants kept right on coming.

"But she's not hurt. Injured! Look at her!"

"I've heard of badly injured people doing things in shock they could never do otherwise."

"Shock!" Father gasped. "People die of shock. Get her!"

"Get in the house, Karen. Run! Lock the door. Pile furniture in front of it. I can't stop these buffaloes."

"David she'll injure herself."

"Shut up Charlie."

I barely made it up the stairs. I slammed the kitchen door and locked it. Jasper, who'd been listening to everything, was right there with a chair. The two of us began creating a barricade, but I felt like David, nothing would stop those buffaloes if they wanted in. I was beginning to feel as though my house were continually under siege.

"I'm all right. Really I am," I kept yelling. "It's all a mistake." I was about out of breath, our furniture is heavy.

The ambulance attendants, by now, were throwing their shoulders against the door.

They were dedicated men.

"You'll end up in a wheelchair just like Jenny said."

"No! No! I'm fine." I tried to calm myself and catch my breath. "I wasn't sick at all. Nothing is wrong with me. Honest. I would never lie to you. It was a ruse to get you here. There's been no accident. No slipped disc," I was getting hoarse.

Father by this time had picked himself off the ground and joined the men at the door. If he were to give the command, the cavalry would have gone out looking for a battering ram. I was trying to think of a good place to hide. "Splintered, Karen. David said 'splintered'. That's worse much worse. We didn't want you to know."

David, by now, had joined the trio on the porch. They were right outside the door shouting and yelling at each other. I don't know about a splintered disc, but the door was beginning to splinter. The furniture would never stand up to the onslaught.

"She has nothing wrong with her disc, Charlie. Her back is supple as a girl's. She even practices yoga. Yoga makes you very young in he back. Stand on your head or something, Karen."

"Weak in the head," one of the attendant snorted. "I don't hold with it."

"Nor do I, son," Father said. "Eastern claptrap. It probably does more harm than good. You have to be careful doing all those crazy twists and things."

"She is careful, Charlie. Very careful. Now calm down everyone." David was out of breath. "I assure you she's in perfect physical condition. Perfect."

"Then what is going on, David? You said…"

"As soon as we send these men away, we'll explain everything, Charlie. I had to lie to you."

"You never lied to me before, David," Father looked doubtful.

"There's a first time for everything." David said.

The ambulance attendant was angry. One of them began to shout again. "I think there's a law against commandeering an ambulance. I could have you arrested."

"You'd have to stand in a long goddam line!" David shouted back.

"If there's nothing wrong why did you get me so upset? I've been frantic with worry. It isn't like you. It isn't like you at all."

"The ambulance wasn't my idea, remember?" David said to the attendant. They'd stopped yelling at each other anyway. "It was his," he pointed at Father.

"Are you trying to put the blame on that fine old gentleman? I don't like what's going on around here."

"I wasn't blaming anyone. I was just reminding you how this started. I didn't call you. He did. He told you all that bull about his daughter, Karen, my wife. It's not true. Not a word of it. What sense would it make to take a perfectly healthy lady to the hospital?"

"We don't know she's healthy 'til we get her there. It's not our job to diagnose."

"No one is sick. No one here ever gets sick."

The attendant snorted again. "Everybody gets sick."

"Or injured. No one fell off her horse. No one broke her neck. All of us are fine. The picture of health."

"You seem a bit breathless, David. When was the last time you had a chest x-ray? You've not started smoking have you?"

"If anyone belongs in a hospital it's him!" David roared.

"David," I spoke softly through the door and all that furniture. "Please stay calm." David made an effort. "Why don't you two guys take that and go back to work? Somebody may really need you back in town. Here." He withdrew his wallet and handed one of men several bills. "If you need more, or if you get in any trouble over this, have someone call me." He gave them the name and telephone number of the minister next-door. "I'll explain everything."

"You better," but they were cooling down. David took one of them by the arm and led him back to the ambulance. The other man followed. David was speaking very slowly. Very softly.

"Karen let me in," Father said.

I peered out the window. David and the men were a safe distance from the house. When I saw them put the stretcher back, Jasper and I started clearing a path and I opened the door. As soon as Father got in I closed and locked it again.

"I still don't understand," I heard one of the men outside say.

"Don't even try," David said.

"But if she didn't fall off that horse how did she get hurt?"

David groaned. He tried again. Finally, the two men still shaking their heads and looking unhappy, climbed back in the cab. They were muttering as they drove away.

David, making his way back to the house, was a shaken man. When he started up the stair, Father said, "David we completely forgot. That's not my luggage. How could those men have made such a stupid blunder?"

He had us there.

*

Father and David lugged all the suitcases into the kitchen and stacked them by the door. Jasper and I put the furniture back. Once Father gets 'thing' in his head it takes weeks to get it out. David tried to call the airport but all the lines were busy. Father turned his nose up at the dozen or pieces of mismatched luggage. "Whoever belongs to that has no taste at all."

"Whoever belong to that is probably mad as hell."

"Airlines today are notorious in their mishandling of luggage."

"How were they in your day, Charlie?"

"Father," I said, "before we start on that, we want you to meet someone."

There would be no dramatic moment. No scenario. No rehearsed lines. Father got it cold turkey. Good old Jasper hadn't said a word during the entire melee. He looked ashen. Observing the scene just lapsed must have been a difficult to do. His coloring would not detract from the story.

Father, when he saw the stranger, donned his most charming smile and extended his hand. "I had no idea we had company, Karen."

"Charlie," David said, "we'd like you to meet your bride-to-be's husband, Jasper Johns Fisher."

After the excitement of the morning the announcement was almost anticlimactic.

*

For the third time in three days Jasper told his story. I'll say one thing for Father, he listened. It was obvious Jasper was not lying. Nevertheless, Father was not giving up without a fight.

"Couldn't resist those big blue eyes, eh?"

"They're the color and size of a big gold coin and you know it."

"She really must have been a knock-out then."

"I doubt she's changed much. Is she wearing the gown with seed pearls? She wore it at her first wedding and when she married me."

"You could have seen that at the museum."

"But I didn't. The museum didn't exist until after we moved up on the hill. Does she still love that big black limo? I had the interior done over to match her eyes and a vanity installed so she could primp. She'll always be a beauty, Colonel."

"Call me Charlie."

"And she'll always be vain."

"You mentioned a man named Barlow. How did he die?"

"He didn't die of natural causes in his sleep." Jasper said. "Jenny, you can bet, had a hand in it. The voice on the phone said the same thing to me that Bobby said when he knocked me on the head."

"You were a pall bearer at the funeral?"

"No. I ran. I won't say it wasn't a cowardly act, but what else could I do? If her arm was so long she could reach Hal all the way up in Vancouver what hope did I have trying to stop her? I didn't even know who my enemies were. I felt what I needed most was friends."

"What if I told you Barlow isn't dead."

"Hal's not dead. My God," Jasper said. He jumped up from the chair and paced the room. "You're not lying to me? You wouldn't do that would you. To trick me? Hal is alive. He's with her!"

"Oh, no, no," Father said "I'm sure not. Jenny's just too smart to do away with such a valuable commodity."

"I want to call him. I want to talk to Hal."

"Sure," Father said.

"Wait, David said. "If that woman's all you say she is, I think you better not try to call him."

"He's right," Father said.

"You saw him. You actually talked to Hal?"

"Big fellow."

Jasper turned. The color left his face.

"Until he stands up."

Jasper grinned. "Charlie don't be tricky. I feel like I've been revived from the dead."

"You have me boy. You have," Father said.

It was delightful watching Jasper come to life, and, beneath that ridiculous wig, Father's mind was clicking along like an abacus.

"But how did they manage the deception?" Jasper asked.

"They probably figured you'd go right to Hal. They were waiting for your call. Probably told him you died at the Mayo. Brought your ashes home."

"But they couldn't have known I knew," Jasper said. "I was careful not to do anything that would make them suspicious."

"You went to a detective."

"That's it," David said. "We forgot to tell you about him. He's blackmailing Karen and me, too. Same guy."

David told Father our story, he hadn't heard that one.

The story on Father's face as the story unfolded was not appropriate to the occasion. I was afraid we'd lost him again. He grinned and the grin grew broader. As the story galloped along into the home stretch, the grin broke into a guffaw. Before David had finished Father was bent double.

I feared for his heart.

David feared for his sanity.

"Why that old snake in the grass. Ace Adams is it now? Does he still look like an over-sized leprechaun minus the hair?"

"He wore a Rudolph Valentine wig," David and I looked at each other.

Father slapped his knee. "That son of a gun. Still got a floozy to pack his gun for him?"

"The very same."

"Well no, I don't suppose it's the same. He used to turn them in every couple of years like a used car. Last one I knew was named Sue Sue. And she was. The original pistol-packin Mama. Couldn't hit her ass with a skillet. Took a shot at Ace once. Missed. Blew a hole in the County Coroner's hat big enough to run a train through. Good thing the Coroner was a pin head."

Father roared. Tears poured out of his eyes. He pulled a white linen handkerchief out of his pocket and mopped at them. His wig was askew.

"Who would believe?"

Certainly not us.

*

It was a charge to see the Colonel and the lumberman grow young before our eyes. Jasper was laughing, too. He couldn't have known what Father knew, but he knew something was afoot, and, to mix a metaphor, what was afoot was going to be good for the cavalry but very bad for the Indians.

"I want the children to stay completely out of this," Father said to Jasper. "Kids running around under foot are nothing but a worry."

"That's exactly what Hal used to say. And he loved his kid, too." Jasper beamed at us.

"You two kids go for a walk. A long walk. The senior members of this firm have work to do."

"Charlie?"

"You, young man, will have your hands full trying to extricate yourself from the mess you've got yourself in. Further you should get that girl to bed, it's a shame the way to treat your wife. Now don't give me any guff. Both of you. Go!"

David was doing a slow burn. It was his house. If Lorraine hadn't knocked when she did, I'm sure there would have been a fight. The meeting between Lorraine and Father was very dramatic. They threw themselves into each other's arms like young, or old, lovers.

"Just the girl we need, Jasper," Father said.

"If it hadn't been for her I wouldn't be here now. "

Father patted Lorraine on her ample rump. "Not to worry little one, Charlie's got this figured. David, you and Karen, take that atrocious luggage back to the airport."

He'd forgotten about my back.

"...maybe that dummy down there has the traffic cleared up by now. Mismanagement. I detest mismanagement. My luggage, ten pieces, is matching cowhide, black and white. My initials and the nametag will identify it for you at any rate. Now don't blunder this time, David, I am a very patient man, but my patience is about to come to an end."

On the way to the airport, David said, "Senility is an interesting phenomenon, Karen. You go in and out of it."

At the luggage counter half a dozen people stood together in an angry knot watching a jet land. Father's matching cowhide was stacked neatly, all ten pieces, at the end of a long counter inside the terminal. David grabbed it and managed to cram it into the back seat of the van. When he was sure no one was looking he opened the tailgate and threw the other pieces out. They lay scattered in a heap at the edge of the curb. He slammed the tailgate shut, jumped in the car. I was driving and we sped off.

"Aren't you going to tell them?"

"They'll turn around eventually. After a day like today I'm in no mood to explain to anybody."

"It has been a day."

"It always is when Charlie's around."

"Well there is one thing."

"Yeah? What?"

"You have to go home and put me to bed." He moved over beside me and put his hand between my legs. We didn't even go into the living room when we got back to the house.

"Did you get it, David my boy?" Father called.

"I did indeed, Charlie."

"Well bring it in."

"I'm putting it to bed."

"Good man," Father said.

Father and Jasper left the next day for Seattle; both of them grinning like Cheshire cats.

Jasper, in a curly blonde Caligula wig, looked ten years younger. Lorraine had cut and dyed one of Father's wigs last night. Long after David and I had gone to bed we could hear them giggling downstairs.

We were noisy but they were noisier.

"It sounds like a nursery school," David said before going to sleep. "What in the hell do you think they're doing down there?"

"Having fun, David," I said.

"Not as much fun as us." David said.

At the airport the next day, Father said, "David I want you to talk to your attorney. You must be able to get out of here for the wedding. I don't care what strings you have to pull. Send me the bill."

David just nodded.

We were standing around in the terminal surrounded by all that luggage when Lew appeared. He hustled his way through the crowd.

"Jesus am I glad I found you guys. You know where them other guys is headed?"

"Where?" David asked.

"Seattle," Lew said. "The three of'em bought tickets to Portland. They're on this afternoon's flight outta Honolulu for Seattle." He looked over at Jasper. "Hey, how's it, Jake? Lorraine told me to tell you she found your fiddle."

I nearly fainted.

Jasper, good man, just grinned.

"That ought to be an interesting flight," David said. He described the three marauders to Father and filled him in on parts of the story Father hadn't heard and then went off to call Ty.

"We'll keep an eye peeled never fear."

"It sounds like Jenny all right," Jasper said.

While we were standing there a goofy-looking individual marched into the area. He gave Father a nasty glare. Father glared back, "I'd fire you in a minute if your mother didn't own the place," he said in his booming best. People turned around. "Should be fired. Runs a lousy outfit."

The man, looking confused and slightly embarrassed, turned his back and walked away.

"Who was that, Father?"

"Some dummy," he replied. "I never forget a face."

David and I were happy when the flight was called. We watched the jet take off, waving the entire time.

"What did Ty say?"

"He sounded happy."

"That's a relief." We hadn't got a parking ticket. The traffic was light all the way home. The ride was beautiful. David was whistling a cowboy song.

We'd have no trouble getting of the island. With all the information pouring in, Ty doubted we'd even go to trial. After the arraignment, which was over in a hurry, I said, "When do we get our money back?"

"Soon. And then you turn it over to me."

"All of it?"

"Most of it," Ty said. "Told you I was one of the lucky ones."
"Thank God," I said, and kissed Ty on the cheek.

The Living Carousel

Father kept us busy the next couple of days running errands and ordering flowers. We depleted the island's supply of plumeria blossoms. All the plumeria trees for miles around looked naked.

We took with us on the place several boxes of ti leaves, red and green, and half a dozen boxes if red ginger and bird of paradise. They'd not be lacking for flowers, but whether it would look like a wedding or a funeral was anybody's guess.

After we got to his house, the flunky Father hired to pick us up looked suspiciously like one of the creeps in the picture Lew got, drove back to the airport to pick up the rest of the wedding paraphernalia.

I spent the evening before the wedding stringing plumier blossom on long willowy bamboo sticks. These enormous sprays were fragrant and everywhere.

Father floated blossoms in all the toilet bowls.

"A little trick I learned from Lurline Roth," he said. I tried to think where he might have met Mrs. Roth.

The blossoms that were left were packaged in plastic bags and stored in a refrigerator to be used instead of rose petals to throw at the bride and groom.

Father's house, on the day of the wedding, was a battlefield. Caterers fought with decorators over space, bartenders fought with waiters over tables. David and I were awakened from what had been an unsound sleep. Those damn geese had honked outside our window all night, by a honking of another sort.

"Without my beautiful flowers who'd eat your lousy food?"

"Then let them eat your absolutely ridiculous floral arrangement. Whoever heard of tie-dyed roses?"

"Gentlemen, gentlemen," we heard Father's voice.

"Gentlemen," David said, and we put our heads under the covers and giggled.

"This is a joyous occasion. We have plenty of room for food and flowers," Father continued. "Please let us not quarrel."

"Well, I'll give him the back of this table but he's got to give me the front."

"If I give him the front there won't be a back."

"Make two displays," Father said.

"Get another table," the caterer advised.

Their voices faded as they moved through the house.

David, who'd extricated himself from under the covers during the rumpus and headed for the bathroom, stuck his head out the door. "How in the hell can you go to the can around here? The goddam things full of flowers."

"Flush them, David, "I said.

Dozens of heavily laden buffet tables and bars were scattered about the house and white-coated waiters carrying horse-trough size buckets of iced-champagne scurried to and fro. They wore white socks over the outside of their shoes so as not to mar the waxed and polished floor.

In one room two huge tables, pushed together, groaned under a mountain of gifts. The wedding party would eat, drink, and smell good. It would also flow, if anyone were sober enough to flow, from room to room, and tray to tray, and bar to bar.

"It's Adams all over again, David said. "Wait'll we get the bill for this."

"Speak of the devil," I poked David in the ribs.

Adams, minus his pistol-packing mama, had followed Father into the room where David and I, chilled and dazzled, stood reviewing our economic ruin.

"Ask one of the boys for a white coat, Ace, me boy. I hope you can find one that fits."

Adams found one. It was two sizes too small. Three inches of Adam's hairy, white, wrists hung out the bottom of the sleeves, and the buttons gaped alarmingly. I wished I had a camera.

"When Jenny and her family shows up pop the first cork. Use these glasses." Father handed Adams a handsome pair of inscribed champagne goblets. I didn't know what Father had on Adams, but it must have been good. If ever there was a boot-licker, Adams was a boot-licker. He bowed. He scraped. He did everything but curtsy, and I expected one at any moment. It was a joy to see. David's color was returning.

The bride's party arrived about a half an hour before the rest of the guests. We'd not been introduced to the Fisher/Woodsbury tribe. Father made some excuse. My back, I guess. Jenny, in her lovely yellow lace, was everything Jasper and Father had said. When she saw me she extended her arms, graceful fingers glittering with blue-white stones and pale pink polish. "I will love you as much as your mother did," her voice tinkled. She was an aging Tinker Bell.

I managed to murmur something.

"David," she turned her golden eyes on my husband and I swear I saw him melt. "I've heard such marvelous things about you. I know we'll be the best of friends. I'll need your help handling Charlie-love," she twinkled up at Father. "We can be allies. Your father-in-law is such a powerful man." She took Father's arm and swayed helplessly, a tiny, dainty, graceful creature, back and forth between them.

I could have killed her.

"I just know we'll all be one big happy family."

Bessie, the monster, my Father's other favorite daughter, and Owen, the lug, and I, were consigned to a colder corner of heaven.

Father introduced us to our new sister and brother-in-law. Bessie began to bray and goofy-jawed Owen lurched forward unsteadily on his feet. Either these two got off to an early start or they were severely retarded.

Bessie's bubble-headed hair-do was dyed bright pistachio nut pink and her peach and satin dress clung to all the wrong spots. It looked as though she'd bought the dress when she was twenty pounds lighter.

Owen put a big fat paw around my waist and felt around. He jumped when Adams popped the cork.

On cue, Jasper appeared in the doorway. He looked elegant in tie and tails. He was a handsome man in his own rugged way, in spite of the curly blonde wig.

"Jenny, my dear, I believe you've met the best man," Father said.

Jenny turned, all smiles and charm. Already she was looking for other fields to conquer. Jasper, with the most courtly bow I've seen since Errol Flynn was bounding across the silver screen, swept the wig from his head like D'Artagnon's feathered hat and said, "The sentiment is returned, Jenny."

That's when the bride fainted the first time.

Bessie and Owen fled.

I wasn't quite sure what to make of the expression on Adam's face. I don't know whether he received a reprieve or a death sentence. Father and Jasper giggled like two dirty little boys behind the barn, and David and I, popping our own corks, toasted the occasion.

The expression on David's face, when the girl he'd raped handed him the bottle, should have been preserved on Mount Rushmore.

"It's the whole damn town," David said.

Father revived his bride with champagne. Iced champagne down the neck does wonders for a fit of the vapors, but he held her tenderly in his arms. When her eyelids began to flutter, Father beckoned Adams and the raped waitress to his side. When Adams leaned over to pour Jenny some wine, as the girl held the glass, Jenny fainted again. I wondered if the poor old lady would make it to the ceremony.

"Wait'll she sees the inscription on the glass," Jasper guffawed.

"Poor little thing," Father winked. "All the excitement's gone to her head.

Later I found the goblets. Etched in pretty Roman script were the words

"'Till Death do us Part"

Jasper Johns Fisher

Charles Warren Skinner

*

When the March through the icy petting zoo began, David and I started last. The truth is we were not consigned to the tail end of the line. We chose it. Bessie and Owen, who'd appeared again for the ceremony, and all Jenny's friends, gathered like vultures at a feast at the forward end.

David and I preferred Lulu.

I have never seen such a dreary collection of human kind.

"Isn't there anyone in this town under sixty?"

"Not if he can help it."

"Why are they all so gray-looking do you suppose?"

"They all go to the same tailor. That's him in the black Hamburg," and sure enough there was a man in black Hamburg and spats, ahead of us in line.

"They all look prosperous."

"We'll have to wait and see them with their clothes off. Anyhow the tailor is also the mortician."

"David," I swallowed a giggle.

"Come on, Karen, don't lag. We're going to miss the show."

We nudged the pair in front of us. It was impossible to pass on the narrow path. The trees in the Christmas tree forest were planted in thick bushy rows.

"Hold on young man. Don't push. Old bones are brittle."

David nodded and took the old lady's arm. I helped steer the old man.

"You folks must be related to the Colonel."

"I'm his daughter."

"I told you, Gerald. I'm Hattie and this is my husband. Gerald. McGuire." We introduced ourselves.

"You're a friend of the bride?" the four of us trotted briskly along.

"Known Jenny for nigh onto fifty years."

David whistled. "Lived in these parts all your life?"

"All our life. But we're beginning to travel a little now we can afford it. Hattie and me went to Bermuda last year."

"On one of those love boat things." Hattie giggled.

"All the boys in town were crazy about Jen when she was girl. Crazy about you, too, Hat."

"She was such a prissy little thing."

"Not like you, hon." The old man gave his wife a squeeze.

"Haven't heard any complaints," she said.

We were yelling at each other now. The sound of the calliope this close to the source was deafening. "Never heard the Wedding March played on a steam calliope before," David said.

"What?" the old man said.

"The music," David yelled. "It's different."

Snow was beginning to fall in thick white swirls. Behind us the animals, still following along, looked like shadows in the forest. When we turned the last turn, we found ourselves in a large circular clearing surrounded by Christmas trees decorated to the teeth. All four of us gasped. We weren't the only ones. Almost all the guests, gathered in concentric rings around the carousel, were stunned.

"I never saw anything like that."

"Have too, Gerald. The merry-go-round at the State Fair. Remember?"

"They weren't real horses."

"But it looked like that," Hattie insisted.

"Used to cost a quarter a ride. Back when a quarter was a lot of money. Only got to ride one once," Gerald said to David. "In my whole life. After a while you get too old."

David stood frozen in awe. Me, too.

The carousel, under an enormous red and gold striped tent that peeked at the top and then swept down to a generous fringe, would have filled Walt Disney's heart with envy. Everything was painted Chinese red and gold and decorated with brightly depicted circus scene and gilded mirrors.

Under the tent in a grand circle of thick fresh cedar chips, eight Isabella Andulusians pranced, manes and tails braided and beribboned, heads checked with bright plumes, hooves painted and ringed with bells.

In all my years with horses I'd only seen one Isabella-colored horse before, and that was in a painting. These animals are a golden yellow with black manes and tails and four black stockings. They're the most remarkably colored animals I had ever seen. Richly colored. It was easy to understand why at one time they'd been called mobile thrones. I didn't even know horses came Isabella colored anymore, and Father had eight of them.

The workings of the carousel was fantastic, the turntable was built on a central platform that revolved around a hub, like a great gaudy wheel lying on its side. There were eight spokes, and at the end of each a barber's pole, suspended on airplane-like wheels, held the device on the ground and made it easy to turn. The whole thing was light as a feather. A little child could have turned it with one finger. Those horses didn't work. They played. It was obvious they loved what they did.

The calliope, a mirrored and rococo affair with an abundance of various-sized gilt pipes, was fake. The music came from a sound system hidden by the midsection of this wonderful toy. The horses were harnessed to a yoke and attached at the end of each spoke. Each animal wore different colored tack with matching ribbons in their manes and tails and a matching feather, proudly upright, between their ears. The horse had been trained to move to the music and stop when it stopped. They pranced and danced, as light as the feathers they wore. A full glass of water wouldn't spill on their backs. They strutted inside that tent as glorious in their movements as they were in their color.

I almost cried it was so beautiful.

"I'd like to meet the guy who designed that," David said.

"They don't even look real, do they, Hat?" The old man said. His face was lighted with a special kind of joy.

The people in the wedding party, still in their drab grays, were as animated as the animals. On their faces was a rosy flush and practical galoshes tap-danced in the snow.

Somebody waved. Somebody hollered. "Now that's what I call a sight!"

When the music and the horses stopped the groom led his bride inside the tent and seated her awkwardly on a horse. She clung to the barber's pole like a frightened little girl, but the sight of this magnificent creation had brightened her spirits.

"Ride'em Jenny," someone called.

"Give us a show, kid," someone yelled.

Jenny waved to the crowd with one free hand while holding tightly to the barber's poke with the other. She tried to smile.

"Don't push, dear. We don't get to ride until the wedding's over," a familiar voice said.

"Why don't you marry me on a thing like that?"

Adams and his blonde were standing about two dozen people to our right. David spotted them the same time I did.

"She should have brought her gun," David said.

"Didn't you see the sign?"

"What sign?"

"The one at the gate. It said, 'Check Your Firearms.'"

The groom detached the horse behind his bride's from the carousel, mounted it, and rode once around the ring, solo, before joining his bride. It was quite a performance. His horse had obviously been schooled in the fine art of dressage. Father just sat there. I was impressed. This animal did a stately passage all he way around the track, capping off his performance with a perfectly balanced levade. Father bowed. So did the horse. It's a pity Father hadn't worn his hat.

The crowd cheered.

Me, too.

After Father's performance, the minister entered and mounted the horse in front of the happy couple, backwards and began reciting the wedding rites. The music started up, a stately waltz this time, and around and around the bride and groom trotted, exchanging vows.

Jasper, looking as pleased as Father, with a short road-shouldered man at his side, stood guard at the entrance to the ride.

"That's the goddamndest sight I ever saw," David said.

When the ceremony was over the music stopped. The groom kissed his bride and carried her off her horse. Everyone cheered. "All right, folks, eight at a time. Don't push. Line up at the gate. The ride's on me. Don't kick these guys. Just sit there. Let the horse do all the work."

"May I go again, Colonel, right side to this time?" the minister asked shyly.

"Lucky seven to begin with, friends. We have a greedy preacher among us."

"Giddy up," the minister said, dismounting and turning around.

Over two hundred people stood in the snow at Father's wedding eager to ride the carousel. Even Bessie and Owen went for a ride. Adams had to battle with the blonde, who was drunk, to get her off the horse, she enjoyed it so much. Call that preacher back," she yelled, "it's my turn."

Lulu

When David had his fill of the carousel innards, I could have spent the rest of my life riding the horse Father rode. We walked back to the house through the forest. We were the last to leave the area.

That's when Lulu attacked David the first time.

She came up behind us, really moving, raced right by me, and kneed David in the ass. Thank God she wasn't full-grown. He flew ten feet in the air as it was.

I managed to catch Lulu by the neck and hang on; she enjoyed the first attack so much she was preparing for the second.

"What the hell hit me?" David groaned. He was knocked silly. If the trees hadn't broken his fall he'd probably have broken all his ribs.

The other animals, goats, geese, dogs and ponies, lined up behind Lulu looking as though they were waiting their turn. Lulu turned her soft brown eyes on me and began to work her mouth.

"Don't spit, Lu babe," I said. "For god's sake don't spit! I love you. David loves you. David," I said softly, "get up quick and head for the house. I don't know how long I can hold this animal. I don't think she likes you. I don't think she likes me, either."

"I hope she doesn't think I care too much for her company either. She damn near killed me. What in the hell'd she hit me with, a crowbar? If I'd turned around you'd have had a little problem on your hands."

"Don't talk, David. Go. Run I can't hold on any longer." Lulu broke away. David ran. But not fast enough. She got him again, and this time, after he was down, she began stomping. The other animals barreled by me, knocking me down this time, in their rush to watch the fun.

"What's the matter with the damn thing? What the hell did I ever do to her?" David managed to get up and started running again.

"She's just a baby, David." I shouted after him. "I think she doesn't like your smell."

I watched David vault the fence between the petting farm and the house. It must have been four and a half feet high. He didn't even graze the top. Good thing, too, Father ran an electric wire along the top. Lulu stopped at the fence and stomped her feet again. I didn't like the look in her eye. This time she looked as thought she wasn't in the least bit particular who she got, as long as she got someone. There was no other someone but me out there.

"There, there, girl," I said, and did some pretty fancy running and fence vaulting myself. I wasn't as lucky a David. I hit the wire, better than Lulu hitting me.

"David," I shrieked, "I got zapped."

"How in the hell does he get any insurance? That damn beast could stomp you to death."

"If you saw the premiums you'd know. Anyway I'd as soon be stomped to death as electrocuted. I was still tingling.

Lulu was stomping and glaring at us across the fence. All the other animals lined up alongside her. They were making unpleasant noises and blowing steam. The music and the crowd must have upset them. I think they were mad we'd got away.

"She just doesn't like you, David. Sometimes that happens." I began to brush the mud and the snow off his clothes and his face.

"You'll have to wash up," I said. "Did you skin your nose? God, you're bleeding." Blood ran in trickles down his face and froze at his chin.

We got inside and while David adjourned to the powder room I got us each a stiff drink. The kid behind the bar was the freakiest-looking thing I ever saw. His arms were too long and his eyes were weird. One was twice the size of the other and they were not the same color. "My God, you're the guy in the picture. The guy at the camp."

The kid winked at me with his one big blue eye. He tried a smile and I wished he hadn't. He had no teeth. Only gums. Mile after mile of big healthy pink gums. "Good party, huh?" he lisped.

I took a deep breath, a big slug of Scotch, and looked around the room.

Shed of their gray and dark-colored overcoats and hats, the people in the room looked almost festive. They were all Father's age though. The only young ones in he room were the waiters and waitresses. The raped waitress walked by carrying a tray of hors d'oeuvres. She offered me one, grinning. "These are real good," she said and pointed to a cheese ball affair studded with shiny green things. "We make them at the home. Miz Fisher, I mean Miz Skinner," she corrected herself with a grin, "got us the recipe."

"What are those," I pointed at the green things.

"Sprouts," she said.

I took a cheese ball and dropped it in a big bowl of flowers. Potato sprouts more than likely, I thought.

Jake, we didn't call him Jasper, when he saw me, came over and introduced me to his friend, Hal Barlow. I liked like the man instantly.

Jake," I said, "Who are all these kids?"

"They're kids from the home," he said. "Your Dad's trying to rehabilitate them."

"Is he succeeding?"

David came into the room, spotted me, and pushed his way through the crowd. His face was badly scratched, and eye was already turning blue. It looked as though it hurt him.

Jake introduced Hal to David. "What's the other guy look like?"

"The other guys has four legs," David said, "and he's a she. The goddam llama attacked me. I was lucky to get out of there alive."

"She really went after him," I said. "For an animals with such beautiful eyes she sure can turn on the dirty looks." I handed David his drink. "I think we should tell Father his llama is mean."

"Oh, he knows it," Jake said. "She attacked me the first day I was here. He usually keeps her penned up. She takes a violent dislike to people. Who knows who or why. I guess in all the excitement he forgot."

"Jesus," David said. "That thing was on our tail through the whole goddam wedding." He took a big slug of whiskey.

Hattie and Gerald McGuire, who looked like Buchwald and Sellers, and who still, minus their heavy overcoats, looked like Buchwald and Sellers, stopped by to say hello and get a better look at David's eye.

"Lovely party," Hattie said.

"How's the other guy?" Gerald ventured.

"His nose is flattened and I bit one of his ears off." David answered.

Hattie gave a happy little squeal.

"That's the way, son. They'll leave you alone if you keep that kind of thing up."

Bessie and Owen passed close by, but I turned my back. What in the hell do you say to people who look like that? "Speak!" "Heel!" "Down boy!" "Sit!"

Adams maneuvered a tray of luscious roast beef by us. David and I grabbed a slice and a hot roll. Adams was still wearing the same white jacket, slightly bloody from all that beef. I hoped. He gave me a big wink as he rolled by. "Looking good, Mrs. Holt," he bowed over the back end off the cart.

His blonde came into the room staggering slightly. She headed in a zigzag path right by us. "Haven't I met you two guys somewhere before?" She didn't stop, but trailed on in somewhat the same direction Adams and the cart took.

We still hadn't seen Father or his bride, my new mother. I almost gagged.

"I think I better go find them," I said. "You stay here, David. I'll be right back. Please don't get lost."

I walked through two rooms packed solid with people. They were beginning to get noisy. I saw an elderly gentleman pitch head first into a crystal punch bowl. Either the excitement was too much for him or the punch exceptionally good, anyway no one paid any attention to him.

The decorator and caterer were still going at it in a corner of the room. "You just take those silly flowers and stick them up your ass," the caterer said and bustled away. He was a roly-poly guy with that disease pygmy women get. His behind stuck out a mile.

The florist was tall and slender. He rolled his eyes to the ceiling. "I'll never work with that fellow again. I say that every time, but this time I mean it." He stamped his foot and minced away.

A lady in front of me swung around unexpectedly, "You're a stupid son-of-a-bitch and if I wasn't married to you I'd divorce you." She poured her drink, ice and all, down my front. "Watch it, dearie!" she said. "And keep your paws off my husband."

A white-coated kid with a tray of champagne glasses passed my way. I grabbed two, one in each hand.

Finally I spotted the groom. He and his bride, who was exhibiting a miraculous recovery, were in the center of the third room, under the wagon wheel chandeliers, holding court. I walked toward them. The husband of the lady who'd poured the drink all over me was following close behind.

"Father," I said. In all the excitement he hadn't seen me enter the room.

"Karen, pet. Friends, I want you to meet my precious daughter, Karen. Doesn't she look well? Amazing powers of recuperation. She broke her back, you know. Just a week before the wedding." I sighed. The back thing was all right, but I was embarrassed by the wet mark down my front. The guy behind me was giving me a pat. Father grabbed me and crushed me to his chest and I spilled the two drinks I was carrying all over myself.

"Karen," Father whispered, "I think you've had enough to drink."

"Your llama just attacked David."

"Nonsense, Karen. Lulu would never attack David."

"Tell that to David. I saw it with my own eyes."

Father looked at me as though he had a hunch about whatever it was I saw with my own eyes, considering the condition I was in.

Jenny, meanwhile, was looking me up and down. Obviously I didn't pass muster.

"A lady spilled her drink on me and Father spilled the other two," I explained and hated myself.

"Of course, dear," Jenny said sweetly.

"And the llama did attack David."

"I'm sure it did."

"Well she did." The man behind me was really beginning to annoy. I'd have bruises on my bottom to explain to David that night.

The raped waitress walked boldly up to Jenny. "Mrs. Raleigh," she began.

"Mrs. Skinner," Jenny said.

The waitress ducked her head. I caught a sly little smile, "Mrs. Skinner," she said it like it was a joke, "Boots wants to know when you'll be leaving. He's afraid the car will overheat if he keeps running it any longer. And that fruit with the flowers," she looked me right in the eye, and Jenny smiled, "wants to know when you want him to pass out the petunias."

"Plumerias."

"Whatevers."

"Now would be fine," Jenny said, and smiling at Father, and me, sort of, moved away with the waitress. They had their heads together whispering. Jenny was obviously mentor to these creeps.

"You be nice to Lulu, Kitten," Father said, "and watch how much you drink. I had no idea you had a drinking problem. Your mother could drink martinis all day in the shade and never spill a drop."

"Of course," I said. I gave up. Jenny was giggling again. Father was bitching. And the old bastard behind me was pinching me black and blue.

"Get a package of flowers now and come see us off."

"You stop and talk to David before you go. Don't you dare go off without seeing him. He's in the room with all the ginger."

The groom blew me a kiss and followed his bride out the door.

A waiter went by with a tall glass of Scotch, it turned out, and water. Plenty of ice. I grabbed it, took a sip, swung around and tossed it, ice and all, in my assailant's face. "You better watch it, dearie," I heard his wife say and was about to run for my life when a tall black man in a white shirt and shiny black shoes appeared at my side. He nodded at me and turned and gave the woman a nasty glare. "I'm Boots," he said. "Your Daddy's chauffer. I want to thank you for sending Jas...I mean Mr. Fiddler...back to us. And I don't want you to worry about your Pap. We're getting this snake's nest cleaned up. My wife's helping in the kitchen so you can bet there won't be games goin' on in there."

"Oh, Boots, thanks a lot." He nodded, and moved rapidly out of the room after the bride and groom and the waitress.

White-coated kids were passing among us now handing out bags of plumeria. I was pleased to note the flowers hadn't turned brown. I took two bags and headed back towards David. My assailant and his wife were gone.

David and Father were shouting at each other.

"That beast should be shot," David said.

"David, my boy, remember your manners. If I didn't know you two better I'd swear you were drunk."

"Look at my face and say that," David's fists were clenched. I was sure he'd never strike an old man, but I hurried over anyway.

"It must have been a misunderstanding."

"Tell that to the fucking llama."

Father's ears were very delicate. He shook his head and walked away.

David was still steaming. "Who in the hell pays the insurance around here?" he asked. I handed him a package of plumerias. "I'd throw them if they were rocks, " he said.

Everybody that could still walk was moving towards the door. The man whose head had been in the punch bowl was carrying on a lively conversation with himself and waving his arms about.

Jenny showed up in a long black sable coat that must have cost a king's ransom.

"Oh, David," I gasped. "Look at that!"

"Just what you need in Hawaii. Ask her, maybe she'll loan it to you."

Jenny took Father's hand and led him out the door. Before and behind us, people were pouring into the snow, lining up on either side of the path the bride and groom would follow. Nobody bothered to put on a coat. They had enough fuel sloshing around inside them to keep them warm through the entire winter. Plumeria blossoms fell like huge white and gold snowflakes around the bride and groom. The air was alive with the sweet-smelling scent of the tropics. The bride and groom were smiling and holding hands, gazing lovingly into each other's eyes.

"They're a pair all right," David said. "As soon as that black hearse takes off so do we."

"Can't we stay just one more day and play on the carousel?"

"Give that crazy beast another crack at me? No. I've had it with this goddam zoo." He waved his arms in every direction."

As the limousine pulled away I could see Father lean over and kiss the bride.

"What do you think's going to happen now, David."

"Who the hell knows? But one thing I do know, she got the worst of the deal."

We went inside, began to pack, and left without saying goodbye to anyone, even Jasper and Hal. I felt sad about leaving that horse.

Within the hour we were on a flight back to Hawaii.

The Scam

It was weeks before we heard from Father. The honeymoon was an extended one. While Father and his bride sailed the Caribbean, David and I rediscovered each other. The rape case against David and me was dropped, the girl came back to the island and admitted her 'error', and, even though the drug trial was still pending, Ty said it was just a formality. Journalists actually came out to see what we had going here, took pictures, and left to write glowing reports for their papers. Dubbed the Couple Who Really Have it Made, for a whole week we were the envy of the island

The windows are back in the living room and the carpet is back on the bedroom floor. David says the water stains on the ceiling, like the pits in the oiled-teak, add character. I've learned to live with them.

His shop is back together, better than ever, the generosity of our insurance company. David whistles his way to work in the morning and does the Holt Beach Scramble on the way home. We haven't had a piece of macadamia-nut-bread for weeks.

Tommy's home on a little R & R, the revolution can be very exhausting, and converting prisoners turned out not to be as easy as he'd thought. I think they drummed him out of the Pen. He really doesn't belong there. The camp people are really sweet to him, but I don't think he made any converts there, either. David threatens to build him a soapbox.

"They're all spoiled, Mom," Tom said to me about the camp people the other day. "Someday those people are going to have to get out in the real world and find out what it's really like out there."

"Why?" I asked him. "You never did."

That made him mad.

Lew solved the beetle problem and we have so many tomatoes Lorraine has incorporated fresh tomatoes in the curry. She still serves chocolate cake, shrimp/tomato curry, and wine, and has convinced herself she's in love with Jasper. His battered old fiddle hangs over the bar right next to a nude done of Lorraine twenty years ago in Papeete.

"Always trust the dolphins," she says cryptically. "They knows a good mans when they sees one."

When Kuuipo called to tell me there was package from the Colonel, I raced into town. Kuuipo had to help me load it in the car. He tried to contain his curiosity, even Hawaiian postmaster must assume a certain amount of professional distance, and nevertheless, I grinned. "I promise to let you know."

"Better you do," he said. He'd been terribly disappointed he hadn't gone to trial. "I'd be the only drug-pushing postmaster in the state," he said shaking his head.

When I got home, David and I opened the box. On its last flight from the islands, it had held thousands of plumeria blossoms. There was still a faint fragrance about it. This time, however, instead of sweet smelling flowers, a half-ton of paper poured out. There were birth certificates, death certificates, a big bundle of those, newspaper clippings and articles, David's and mine among them, legal documents, deeds, titles, wedding certificates. Papers, papers, and more papers.

We put everything back in the box, put the lid on, and stashed it under David's new desk.

Father's letter of explanation, typically, arrived two days later. It was written at the zoo. I read it aloud.

"Children," Father began, "I want you to store the papers in a safe dry place. Get a safe. Do NOT place them in a bank or institutional vault. Jenny says those bastards peek."

"They did at her bank anyway, "David said.

"Either buy a safe large enough or have David design one. David is very good at designing things even though he is a slight bit impractical. He should consider working to improve the practical side of his nature.

The check for a quarter of a million…"

I dropped the letter but David beat me to the envelope. He shook it and a check fell out. I caught it. We both looked at the figures, stunned.

"He should have got a bigger check. There's not enough room for all those zeros."

"…is a gift to you kids from your new mother." I continued reading. "She paid the taxes so it's all yours. Have fun! It should be enough to pay you back for all the help you gave me during my time of need. But don't ever forget, that's what families are for! Someday you may have to ask your children for help."

"And Tommy will send the organizers. Pat will send the locals. And Alice will rob a bank."

"But they'll do it for us, Karen, and that's all that counts."

"…and Jenny also paid my bills. How friendly those dummies are when they've got your money-so that should not concern you any longer. She's as bad as David, but I still believe you can

212

teach an old dog new tricks. Anyway she has a lot more money than they do."

"She won't have it long." David said.

"Maybe he's changed his ways."

"Charlie? And the universe is shaped like a three-corned hat."

"Oh, David, someone told you."

David nodded.

"You're not mad?"

"Hell, no. Like the ceiling and the floor it adds character."

"Well don't get carried away, we still have horses to feed."

"You have horses to feed."

I read on. 'My bride has also, very generously, turned Fish's company over to me. Jasper runs it. And owns it. Those papers are included. No one here except Bessie and Owen and Boots and Tildy caught on. Oh, yes, Bessie and Owen have moved on. Jasper calls himself Jake Fiddler."

" Oh, that's cute" I said.

"Remember that. In his will he left the company to David and Hal's kids. Jake thought it fitting. He needs a family and I'm sure they are just about as good as any other."

"That's nice to know," David said.

"Don't feel left out, Karen, you don't need a lumber empire. All little girls should be so rich."

"Jen also paid off the mortgage here and this I want you to have, Karen. I know you'll take good care if the animals. Be sure you select good vets. All I ask is that you do not dismantle the carousel I designed..."

"He designed it?" David said awed. "There is no end to the man."

"...and that you give the animals a home for the rest of their little lives. They were good friends to your father, Karen, during very lonely and bad times."

"There! Not here! All I need is that goddam Lulu stomping around in the bush. I'd never get to work," David said.

"Father's going to out live all of them. Us too," I said, "so don't worry."

"He will if he's careful what he eats."

"Jenny had grandiose plans for a shopping center here. Had it all set up. Millions of dollars involved but I put a nix to that. I'm trying to turn the place into a children's park. Don't worry, if that happens you'll get money, it won't be a gift to the state. I want the park to be called the Charles Warren Skinner Children's Playground and Zoo and I want a statue of me erected down by the carousel. Am having sketches done now.

Sold that damn barge Jenny was driving. Bought a bright red Masaratti. It's turning her on, I can tell, although she won't admit it. Am teaching her to ride, too. You're never too old. Am sending Boots, our driver, to cooking school. His wife's good but she needs both eyes to keep on top of what goes on in that kitchen..."

In spite of ourselves we laughed.

"Never be too quick to judge people, children, especially old folks. And don't ever laugh at a second childhood. Some of us never got a first one. Really think Jen is beginning to get some real fun out of life. About time. You know, of course, she really isn't seventy-five. But that's all right since I'm not really eighty.

Getting rid of Bessie and Owen, that pair of dummies, helped. Ace arranged for their departure. Good man to have on your side, children, don't forget that either. By the way he married his blonde. Her name's Flo. That ought to settle him down a little. Unlike Jenny and me, Ace never did grow up. Oh, the stories I could tell you about Ace."

"Oh, Charlie," David groaned, "the stories I could tell him about you."

"Bet? Ace probably knows more about Father than we do. Wouldn't you love to know what those two were up to? Wonder if Ace and Flo got married on the carousel?" I read on.

"We are really trying to rehabilitate those kids in Jen's juvenile home. That's one debt she owes and I'm going to see she pays it. Poor little tykes. Most of them never had much of a chance either. That little girl you didn't rape, David, is really great with animals. Surprised to discover lots of them are good with animals."

"Especially Lulu," David said. "The little girl I didn't rape would understand her. She'd love her."

"David are you still mad at that poor little llama?"

"Tell Lorraine Jake sends his love. Hopes to be over soon. We're living in the house on the hill. That goes back to Jake, if we go first. I think he and Jenny may even learn to be friends but he still never comes to dinner."

Both David and I roared.

"But he takes us out a lot. He has a place in town. Still wears the same wig. For luck. But I'll get him going on some really good ones. We're doing a lot of cleaning up in that town. Think Jake will run for Mayor. At least we'll get rid of those ninnies Jenny had in office. The town was a real mess let me tell you.

Jen's got a mind for business that's for sure but she's a terrible judge of character.

Write to your dear old father. And your new mother. You'll learn to love her, children. Wait and see. Oh, yes, I want you to get Jenny a real Hawaiian muumuu. She wears a size six. Get Lorraine to do that, Karen, your taste is much too conservative for Jenny. Jenny says if she could spruce you up some you'd be a real beauty, Karen. When we come over you two will have to go shopping."

"I hope Lorraine puts her in one that glows in the dark. Spruce me up! I'll spruce her up. I'll put her on Malcolm and put a burr under the saddle."

"Karen."

I wrinkled my nose.

"All is well. Take care of your back, Kitten. And if that ornery horse ever throws you again I better not hear about it. Nothing worse than an untrustworthy animals."

"You know what, Karen?"

"What, David?"

" You have a very interesting father."

I giggled.

"I love both of you very much. See you soon."

He signed it, " Father."

I put the letter back in the envelope with the box of papers. We'd find a place to store the box later. Maybe Ty could help us out here.

"You know what I think is kind of sad," David said looking at the check.

"What?"

"Well, that I'll probably never get another piece of macadamia-nut-banana bread. That was good stuff, Karen."

"Oh but you will, David."

"No. Never."

"Sure you will. When Father and Jenny come calling and Jenny makes the soup I'll make the bread."

"That's not funny, Karen, "David said.

"Who's laughing? There is absolutely nothing funny about a piece of macadamia-nut-banana bread."

Together, David holding the check in one hand and my hand in the other, we set out for home.

It was a beautiful day on Kauai.

-end-

Made in the USA
Charleston, SC
05 December 2011